# THE LAST DAYS OF CHRISTMAS

### BROTHERHOOD PROTECTORS WORLD

STACEY WILK

Twisted Page Press LLC

*To Kimberley and Lori*
*Your friendship was the best gift in the most unexpected*
*way. Thank you for filling the journey together with*
*laughs, love, and the occasional fire alarm.*

BROTHERHOOD PROTECTORS

ORIGINAL SERIES BY ELLE JAMES

# CHAPTER 1

ZANE CUTLER WANTED a hot shower and a hot meal. His shoulder ached from the cold December night and all the kids he helped climb onto Santa's lap. He shoved out of his pickup with the Santa jacket in his fist and let out a long breath. The Christmas decorations on his front lawn never looked so good. Snow fell in circular gusts. He loved Christmas.

Gerald Avenue had three weeks until Winter's annual Christmas Light Competition. If they were going to win the Best Street category, every house needed to be decorated. He had a problem. Not every house was. Gerald Avenue had to win. He won—at everything.

He held the title in the Best House category five years in a row. The falling snow added an extra appeal to his display. His votes would go up on the Facebook page after tonight. Nothing his neighbor across the street, Davis Eberstark, could do would change that. Zane turned for his house and stopped.

An unexpected surprise sat in the driveway of the vacant, dark house next door. A car that wasn't there this afternoon. Considering the later hour and the predicted snow fall for the night, the house must've been rented. He zipped his coat to his neck and smiled. The meal and the shower could wait. He would stop next door and explain to his new neighbor the importance of the competition, but not without the flyer. He wanted to look official. Gerald Avenue was still in the running.

The doorknob of his front door turned under his touch. He suppressed a growl. "Sloane, you have to keep the door locked." He tossed his keys on the table by the door, and dropped the jacket to the Santa suit and his parka on the bench.

His sister appeared in the kitchen doorway with her black hair falling around her face, a shine on her nose, and her bare feet poking out of wide-legged jeans. "I forgot. Dinner will be ready in about five minutes."

She blew the hair away from her face and marched back into the kitchen before he could say anything else. He followed and grabbed the flyer with the information about the Christmas light competition. "I'll be right back," he said.

"Where are you going?" She tasted her sauce cooking on the gas stove in her big cast iron pot.

The whole room smelled of tomatoes and garlic. His stomach growled.

"I'm dropping this off to the new neighbor." He waved the green paper.

"Honestly, Zane, they just moved in a few hours ago. Give them a chance to get settled before you go banging on the door about that contest you love so much."

"Did you see them?" Another family probably moved in. The street and the small town were a good, safe place to raise kids. He lived in Winter for those reasons too even though he didn't have kids of his own. He wasn't sure if it would ever happen, and he was okay with that. He had his niece to spoil.

"I only saw the car in the driveway when I went out to meet Cleo's bus. How's the shoulder?"

"Hurts like hell. I'll be right back." He had fallen off Mrs. Schroeder's roof helping her hang lights. The octogenarian was as competitive as he was and wanted to take the Best Street prize too, but she wasn't as nimble as she used to be.

His team at the Brotherhood Protectors laughed for a week when they found out he rolled off the roof onto the ground. He wanted to knock them all out, but his arm had hurt too much.

"Don't you want to change out of your costume?" She indicated his Santa pants and boots with her wooden spoon. Her eyebrow climbed into her hairline.

3

"Who can resist Santa? Thanks for making dinner."

"You're cleaning up. I have a meeting tonight." Her words chased him down the hallway and out the door.

The cold air bit the skin on his bare arms. He should've grabbed a coat. He hurried across the lawns and knocked on the front door of the old Victorian. A few cars drove by and slowed down in front of Davis' house. Tomorrow he would add more decorations to his own house. He couldn't allow Davis to get ahead in the poll. He knocked again and rang the bell.

The creak of a door on rusty hinges tore his thoughts back to the neighbor's front porch. Whoever was on the other side opened it only a crack.

"Can I help you?" A soft, female voice drifted through the opening.

He couldn't see who was on the other side of the door. The lights behind her were out and the rooms were dark. He positioned himself to the side of the door.

"Hi. I'm Zane Cutler. I live next door. I came to welcome you to the neighborhood and tell you about our annual Christmas light competition."

"Thanks, but I'm not interested." She started to close the door.

"Hang on a second. I brought over the information." He slid the paper through the opening hoping she would open the door wider, but she did not. She didn't even take the paper.

"It's a big deal. Everyone on the street participates." He wanted her to at least look at it. The cold night froze his ass off and made his shoulder ache more.

"Mr. Cutler, you've come at a bad time. If you'll excuse me." She tried to close the door again.

"I don't mean to bother you. I guess I should've waited to stop by, but the sooner you know everyone on the street decorates their house for Christmas, the sooner you can get started. We always win. We're the best street in the town." That wasn't any accident either. He'd been grooming every resident for years.

She opened the door wider. He had her. The front porch light cast its glow on her long brown hair that framed her face. She stared at him with one eyebrow arched and her hand on her hip. Her lips, absent of a smile, were pressed together, but he couldn't miss her full bottom lip. He suspected she was more beautiful when she smiled.

"Will you at least take the flyer?" Her lawn would be decorated in no time. He would even offer to help just to see if she might smile at him.

"I'm not interested in participating in any competition. Thank you for stopping by, but if you don't go now, I'll be forced to call the police." She stood as tall as his chest and had to tilt her chin to look up at him.

Her gaze never wavered from his, but she didn't close the door.

"Anyone at the police department can vouch I'm not crazy. Besides, I'm the Santa down at the hospital." He pointed to his red baggy pants tucked into black boots. Too bad he hadn't thrown on the jacket too. No one could say no to a Santa.

"If I take that paper, will you go?"

He detected a hint of a smile. That was all he needed to score. He leaned against the doorjamb and crossed his ankles. "I'll go when you agree to string some lights on the tree in your yard."

She held out her hand. "I will agree to no such thing. I don't even like Christmas. But if taking your piece of paper will make you go, I'll be happy to do that."

"Are you Jewish? Because it's okay if you are. The Horowitzes down the street don't celebrate Christmas, but they decorate with Hanukkah stuff just so the street can win." He hadn't considered she might not celebrate. Stupid on his part. His sister would say he was insensitive. Which he was not.

"I just don't like Christmas. Please give me the paper."

He began to hand it over but stopped. "Why don't you like Christmas?"

"Why do you ask so many questions?" She rubbed her arms. The cold was probably getting to her too, but she still didn't slam that door in his face. He was gaining ground.

"I like to know about my neighbors." Asking questions made him good at his job with the Brotherhood Protectors. The more he knew about a client, the better he could keep them safe.

She let out a long breath and stared at the porch ceiling. He was pressing his luck. She would probably call the police on him, but he couldn't seem to stop himself. His curiosity had the best of him. And he liked a challenge. Especially one as attractive as she was.

"I'm not very interesting. I'd like to get back inside and finish unpacking. Thank you for stopping by."

He eased closer and handed over the flyer. The scent of cinnamon filled the space between them and took his mind off the cold. "You never told me your name."

"I did not."

"Well, it's nice to meet you anyway." He'd come back tomorrow with cookies or his niece. No one could resist a cute five-year-old either.

She snatched the flyer from his grip. "Good night, Mr. Cutler."

"Call me Zane." Her quick move captured his attention and made his insides prickle with intrigue.

He trotted down the front steps, but he wasn't

done with his pretty new neighbor. He had a competition to win, and he never lost.

"My name is Faith." Her soothing voice settled on his shoulders mixed with melting snowflakes.

He stopped and turn with deliberation. "It really is nice to meet you, Faith. Welcome to the neighborhood."

She closed the door and turned off the porch light. Oh yeah, he'd have her house decorated by the week's end.

# CHAPTER 2

FAITH LEANED against the front door and waited for her heart to slow. She hadn't expected anyone to knock so late. She wasn't expecting anyone to knock at all. Least of all a handsome and charming man in half a Santa suit.

She could relax. No one had found her. For now. Because at some point it would happen. It happened before. She was on borrowed time. Always had been. Her luck had to run out eventually.

She glanced at the flyer still fisted in her grip. "No, thanks, Mr. Cutler. If Christmas never came again, it would be too soon," she said to herself.

Zane Cutler seemed to be a man used to getting what he wanted. Even though she would not participate in some silly decorating competition, she had handed over her name without much fight.

She crumpled the paper and tossed it in the trash.

Her muscles ached from lugging moving boxes today. Everything she owned she dragged inside the nineteen-hundred's Victorian house by herself. This new place, cute as it was with small rooms full of character and charm, would get her through until spring, then she'd move on again. Stay six months at a time. No more. No roots.

With a tea kettle up for boiling, she plopped herself on the couch to bang out a few thousand words on her latest romance novel that was due to the publisher by the first week of January. That gave her roughly four weeks to finish or flush her career down a dentist's sink with too much gritty toothpaste.

She tried to keep her mind on her work, but images of her new neighbor snuck in and knocked her concentration off-balance. That black t-shirt hugged his chest in all the right places. He filled up most of her doorway with his broad shoulders and height. She let out a long breath. It had been a long time since she'd been in a relationship. She almost missed the emotional intimacy. Almost. Not enough to reveal her secrets to anyone. She wouldn't mind a little sex, though.

Her phone chirped next to her, and the tea kettle tooted its horn at the same time. She grabbed the phone and ran for the small kitchen with not enough cabinets or enough space for a kitchen table. "Hey, Molly."

"How's the new place?" Molly's loud voice banged around inside her head. She put the phone on speaker.

"It's cute. Thank you for finding it." Molly had been willing to rent home after home without questions. She appreciated the help because Molly was her literary agent and not a real estate agent. She trusted Molly more than anyone.

"It's the least I could do for my favorite client." Molly said that to all her clients.

"I am very grateful for all the real estate moves you've helped me with." She pulled the kettle off the flame, and the whistle faded to a whimper.

"Well, I'm glad because you aren't going to like what I'm about to say." The chirpiness dropped out of her voice as if Santa dropped an elf on its head.

She sagged against the counter. The laminate corner poked her side. She did not want to hear bad news this time of year. She could barely handle Christmas when things went well. "Shoot it to me straight."

"The publisher wants the edits done by Christmas Eve."

"That's twelve days sooner. Why?" She needed every one of those days to finish the book. She had handed in a novel with a strong beginning, and a decent ending, but nothing in the middle. Her editor wasn't happy about it.

"They have an author they want to push out on the January fifth date."

"A bigger seller." Something she struggled with recently. The publisher always backed the winning horse. The reality that it wasn't her any longer burned her.

She sloshed the hot water into a green mug she found in the cabinet. Thankfully, the house came mostly furnished. Her measly belongings wouldn't fill a whole room.

"I'm afraid so. It's John James. His thirteenth thriller, which was supposed to be out this past October, is finally ready for release. They don't want to wait any longer. They need to hit numbers. They want to release your book two days before."

"They want to rush edits? Are they crazy? They can't do that." The tea burned her tongue.

"They can, and they will."

Her book sales had been taking a dive. They had already threatened not to take any more books in the series. If she didn't make this new deadline, it would be career suicide.

"There's one more thing," Molly said.

"What else?" She grabbed onto the counter for support.

"They want to meet Mac Addison."

"Oh no. Absolutely not." Her heart beat picked up speed. She tried to take a few slow breaths, but that didn't help. Holding onto the kitchen counter wasn't enough support. She found a chair in the dining room and dropped down on it.

"They want to find a marketing angle for the guy who writes successful romance novels. If Mac Addison is likeable, especially on camera, the publisher can push for a film deal. You could be the next Nicholas Sparks."

"I can't do it. How would I even do it? No, it will kill my career. Part of the interest in Mac Addison is no one has ever seen him. Talk them out of it. It's what I pay you for."

She had built a career on anonymity. No one knew she was Mac Addison, and she liked it that way. If her face was linked to the international best seller there wouldn't be a place in the world she could hide from her parents' murderer.

"You pay me for selling your books. What if we got a guy to pretend to be Mac?"

All her hard work, years of writing books and garnering readers and good reviews, would instantly go to some guy playing a role. She couldn't have a stranger becoming the face of her business. If she couldn't sit in front of the camera herself, no one would have to pretend to be Mac Addison. If she didn't have to hide her past, there never would have been a Mac Addison.

"No guy. I'll have the book to you by the twenty-fourth. I have to go." She ended the call without waiting for Molly to say another thing.

She tossed the phone on the table and went to the window. The handsome neighbor's house and some of the street could be seen from here. Christmas decorations brightened every front lawn. Snow fell through the glow of the street lights and dusted the ground. Hopefully, more neighbors wouldn't come banging on her door with gifts of fruitcake to persuade her to put up lights because she wouldn't.

She ran through the list of possibilities on how to keep Mac Addison hidden and didn't like any of them. The wind howled against the house, voicing its opinion about Christmas. A shiver ran over her skin.

All she had to do was finish her book and stay away from Zane Cutler. He was too nosy with all his questions and maybe too charming to resist answering. As long as nothing went wrong, she'd hand in her final book, and Mac Addison would tell the publisher he was going into hiding.

Forever.

# CHAPTER 3

FAITH FOUND a shovel in the garage. She had come up for air after working all day on her book with tired eyes and a kink in her neck. Fresh air would do good to clear her head, and the sidewalk needed clearing before the sun completely set and turned her front walk into an ice skating rink.

She wrapped her wool scarf around her neck. The shovel scraped against the pavement with each heave. Her body heated up inside her parka, but the physical labor was a much-needed change from sitting at her desk all day absorbed in her story.

The sun dipped below the tips of the Montana mountaintops and painted the sky with translucent pinks and grays. Nighttime would soon spread its darkness like a black cloak over the shoulders of the town. She wanted to be inside in front of the fire before that happened. These first few days in the town of Winter had given her the quiet she longed for. No one else had come by to welcome her to the neighborhood.

She stole a glance at Zane's house and ignored the tinge of disappointment that he wasn't outside. Her mind wandered over the memory of his black hair curling at the base of his neck. A speckle of beard dusted his strong jaw. The Santa pants were cute.

He had returned one more time to ask her to decorate her yard. He really wanted to win that competition, but she held her ground. No lights or mistletoe for this lady. Boycotting Christmas had become her mantra. Celebrating Christmas was for people who had loved ones around to share it with. That wasn't her. Fantasies were safe, but a real man in her life was trouble. She would be better off forgetting Zane and his confident smile.

While she allowed thoughts of her neighbor to occupy her mind, the sun sank further behind the mountains. The colors washed out of the sky, leaving everything dull and lifeless. The bare branches swayed in the early evening breeze like tentacles of a winter monster. She needed to hurry up and made her way around from the front of the garage to the porch wielding her shovel. A red object stopped her mid-swing.

An envelope lay on the mat by the front door. She glanced over her shoulder, but the street was empty except for the occasional inflatable snowman rocking in the wind or Santa in someone's yard. The neighbors were probably inside eating dinner in the safety of their warm kitchens. Many of the houses were lit by the glow of indoor lighting. The wind blew cold against her face as if to whisper, "Who left the card?"

She stood over it, debating on picking it up or leaving it. The envelope was addressed to her, but there was no return address or stamp. She broke out in a sweat under her heavy coat and berated herself. It was probably just a season's greetings from another friendly neighbor. They were in Montana. People were nice in small towns. Except no one knew her name besides Zane. The house was rented in Molly's name.

She retrieved the envelope and slid the card out. The front was beige with a drawing of a Christmas tree. "A Christmas Wish for You" was printed in red script to the right. The card was simple and something found in any greeting card store.

The message on the inside turned her blood to ice water.

*We know who you are.* Was the only thing written in black ink.

She spun around checking for anyone who might be standing on the sidewalk or lurking in a bush, but the street remained silent. The inflatable snowman continued to sway in the wind. The smile on his face made her think of Jack Torrance from *The Shining*. She grabbed the shovel with shaking hands and ran.

The garage door made a slothful descent, giving a stalker plenty of time to dive under it and get her. Her breath came in short bursts, and her heart demanded to be released from her chest while she waited for the door to meet the concrete. She hurried through the house and checked that all the doors and windows were locked. Her hand hovered over her phone, ready to call the police.

"Stop it." The echo of her voice against the walls of the small kitchen shook her back into reality.

The card meant nothing. It could be from anyone. She had been careful and covered her tracks well. The holidays had her out of sorts along with the request from her publisher to meet Mac Addison. Everyone knew a move was stressful, and she had moved twice this year. She admitted to being a little paranoid, but that's what had kept her alive. She didn't want to end up like her parents. Especially not at Christmas.

She shrugged out of her coat and flopped down on the couch in the living room. The room was dark, but she wanted it that way since it faced the front of the house. She needed to pull herself together. Her imagination got the best of her.

But what if they had found her? Then what did she do? Who would help her stay safe? She'd be fine. She was being ridiculous. A small deranged laugh escaped her lips. Yeah, she was losing it.

Muffled voices accented the darkness outside.

Her spine snapped straight. She peered over the back of the couch and out the window. The lack of light inside gave her cover, but the snow on the ground provided a little light outside. Someone was out there. Two people stood on her lawn.

She couldn't make out any details, but the two people appeared to be men. They stood facing each other. One man's arm punctuated the air. She watched for what seemed to be an hour but was only minutes. The men moved around in her yard but didn't come near the house.

She didn't care. They didn't belong. They were trespassing. If they were the killers, it would be best for them to have a run-in with the police and not with her. She doubted her shovel would be much of a weapon.

She dialed 9-1-1.

## CHAPTER 4

"Davis, hold the lights while I wrap them around the tree." Zane positioned a ladder on the side of the tree furthest from Faith's house.

The house was dark as ink. She probably wasn't home. He hoped she liked the surprise when she saw it. She had been determined to tell him no the last time they spoke.

"I don't know about this. Are you sure this is a good idea?" Davis fed the lights to him while he shook his head.

The man hadn't loved his idea of coming over and decorating Faith's house. They weren't going to touch the house. Only the three trees closest to the road. Nothing in the rules about the light competition said a street couldn't win if the lights were only on the trees. They would have a better chance if she decorated the house too, but this would do for now.

He still had time to convince her to hang a wreath on the door.

"It's for the contest." Every time he wrapped the wire around the trunk, his shoulder ached.

"You should've asked her first." Davis shook his knit-hat-covered head again.

"Once she sees how great the street looks all lit up, she'll come around. We can say it's a house warming present. Don't women love those kinds of things?"

"Flowers would work better." Sarcasm froze on Davis's words.

"Just keep handing me lights. We're almost done." They would have to test them to make sure they worked. He would have to run an extension cord to the house to plug them in, but one task at a time.

He wondered what kind of gifts his new neighbor liked and who would be giving her some this Christmas. So far, he hadn't noticed any other cars coming or going from her place. Maybe there wasn't a man in her life because he certainly wouldn't want to be away from the woman he loved at Christmastime. Not that he'd had a woman recently. Not since the divorce.

A car sped down the street, throwing up blue and red lights all over the place. The vehicle skidded to a stop on an angle in front of Faith's house. Zane climbed down off the ladder and met the officer pushing out of the vehicle.

"You've done it now," Davis said.

"What's going on?" he said. The police in Winter didn't have a whole lot to do. Especially not on his street.

"A disturbance was called in. I'm here to check it out." Officer Bud Lewis was the senior officer on the force. He had the gray hair to prove it.

"I didn't see anything. Did you, Davis?" He might be on leave from the Brotherhood Protectors for his shoulder injury, but he was still good at what he did, and he would've noticed something happening on his street that didn't belong there.

"Howdy, Bud. How's your dad doing?" Davis shook Bud's hand.

"Still driving my mom crazy. Davis, did Zane here talk you into helping him?" Bud adjusted his hat and fisted his hands on his hips.

"What are you getting at?" Davis said.

"You're the disturbance, Zane." Bud raised an eyebrow and cracked a smile.

"Me? What are you talking about?" He knew exactly what Bud was talking about. He wasn't going to give him the satisfaction.

"The resident called in a complaint about two men in her yard. As soon as I pulled up and saw you, I knew. You aren't going to win this year no matter how many lights you put on everyone's trees. My street looks better than this pathetic street does. No offense, Davis. Your house looks great. Better than

22

Zane's piece of shit." Bud slapped him on the shoulder and had himself a good chuckle.

"None taken." Davis smirked.

"You're going to eat those words." He and Bud had been competing since their days on the high school baseball diamond.

"Have you seen Lincoln Smith's street? You don't stand a chance."

"He's got like three houses over there. It shouldn't even be allowed in the competition." Linc lived at the top of the mountain on a quiet road. He wouldn't let Linc beat him this year when Gerald Avenue had twenty houses. Even if Faith didn't let him leave the lights, his street was better than Linc's.

"Are you going to say that to his face?" Bud said.

"Linc? Are you crazy? He'll kick my ass all over the place. Now you, on the other hand, are a different story."

"Don't go getting ahead of yourself. I've got to report what I found out here since I had to get up from my crossword puzzle to investigate. You have to take your lights and go home or I'll have to arrest you and that would give me great pleasure." Bud pulled out his handcuffs and waved them.

"Good night, gentleman. This old man is going home to some warm soup and cocoa. I've got more decorations to add tomorrow. I don't need something like an arrest to mess up my plans." Davis waved and headed up the street.

"Davis, don't let him scare you. He's all talk. He doesn't have the balls to arrest me." He turned to Bud. "Did she really call you?" So she was home and checking out the window. He stole a glance in that direction, but didn't see her. She could've come out and said something. She didn't need to call the police, but it's what he would've wanted Sloane to do.

"You've scared her pretty good. She's new and doesn't know anyone. That didn't occur to you?" Bud silenced the radio on his hip.

"I was doing her a favor." Maybe sneaking on the yard was going too far, but it was for the sake of the competition. He would have to make her see that.

"You want to win. I know it's not your style, but ask permission next time you mess around on a lady's property in the dark. Do you want to go to her door and apologize, or do I have to? Because if I do, then I've got to write a long report that will piss me off. If you do it, I can say I surveyed the area, and there was nothing happening."

"I wouldn't want you to have to do your job." He wanted another excuse to speak to Faith anyway.

"Good. I'll see you at the Christmas Eve party at the Weston Ranch?"

Ty Weston and his family hosted an annual Christmas Eve party for most of the people in the area. All of the Brotherhood who lived in a three-hour radius came. He would be no different. Especially since Lincoln Smith was Ty's brother-in-law and Linc was his squad leader on assignments that required a team.

"I'll be there." Maybe he could bring a date. He stole another glance at Faith's house.

"Going solo this year. Unless Sloane would like to go." Bud walked back to the squad car. He had recently divorced. Bud was a good man and a good friend. He would have no problem with Bud dating Sloane.

"I don't get involved in my sister's love life. You'll have to ask her yourself." Sloane wasn't ready to date yet. She was too busy raising Cleo. He could let Bud find that out for himself on the off-chance Sloane did go out on a date with him.

"She always turns me down. Don't forget to apologize to your neighbor. I'll check to see if you did. And take those lights down." Bud hitched a leg into the car, turned off the lights, and pulled away.

He wasn't taking the lights down, but he would apologize. Now was as good a time as any, and he knocked on the door. She didn't answer.

He knocked harder this time. "Faith, it's Zane. Please open up."

He wasn't sure she heard him. Tired of standing out in the cold, which only managed to make his shoulder ache even through his coat, he stepped off the porch.

The door swooshed open. "Hi." Her voice was soft and small.

"Hey. I wasn't sure if you were home."

She stepped out onto the porch and rubbed her arms. Her gaze took in the street before settling on him. "Did you see anyone in the yard? I called the police, but they never showed up."

He took off his hat and scratched his head. "About that. Um, the police were here."

Her eyes grew to the size of an igloo. "You saw them? Why didn't they check on me? What kind of a town is this?"

"The kind where they know everyone. I spoke with Bud. That's Officer Lewis."

She threw her arms in the air. "Oh, I get it. He sees you and decides if there was a problem you would've noticed it. I must be a hysterical female who overreacts. Is that how it goes?"

The defiant tilt of her chin and fire in her voice warmed his insides. He unzipped his coat and arranged his face into a humble smile. "I was the problem."

"Excuse me?" She took a step back out of the porch light. Shadows crossed her worried face.

"I was stringing lights around your trees." He held his palms up. He hadn't meant any harm. She had to see that.

"What's the matter with you?"

"They are only a few lights on the trees by the street. Why are you so upset?" That wasn't an apology.

26

"Men like you think the whole world revolves around them and everyone should do what you want. I told you no, but that's not enough. You bully your way onto my property and put lights on my tree without permission."

"Hey, I'm sorry if I scared you. The lights are for the competition. The poll is already up on Facebook. Residents of the town are starting to leave comments about which streets are still in the dark. We've won five years in a row. We can't lose."

"I don't want decorations in my yard. If you had stopped to think about something other than winning your contest, you might have realized I meant what I said." She clenched and shook her fists.

"I can admit I was wrong to come over here before asking if you minded. That was a little over the top, but I'm not an asshole." The whole evening had spun out of control. She wouldn't let him apologize. He didn't want her mad at him. The opposite in fact. He liked it when she smiled at him.

"Please go. It's cold out here, and I'm tired." Any trace of a smile was nowhere in sight.

"I really am sorry."

"Whatever. Just take your lights with you." She waved a hand in the air and turned to go.

"Why won't you accept my apology?" He grabbed her wrist before she could scoot away from him. Her skin was soft and warm under his touch.

"Apology accepted." She dropped her gaze to his hand, and he released her with some regret.

"Do you want to get some coffee?" The words had slipped out without any preparation.

"No, I don't. I have work to do."

"What kind of work?"

"Good night, Zane." She closed the door.

There was something provocative about this woman and her dark smoldering eyes that gripped his attention. Since the first time they met, his mind continuously wandered to her, wondering what she was like or what would make her laugh. He imagined she had a beautiful laugh.

"I won't take no for an answer." He called to the closed door.

She turned off the light. He laughed. His pretty new neighbor presented a showdown. Nothing he liked better. If she had been severely upset with him, she would've slammed the door in his face and called the police back. But there was something going on with her. It might've been the way her hands were shaking the entire time they spoke or the way her gaze bounced around. The thought of trespassers in her yard shook her up quite a bit. He wanted to know why.

"Uncle Zane." Cleo came running across the lawn and threw herself against his legs. She wrapped her arms around his waist.

"What are you doing out here, kiddo?" He

squatted down to look at her. The buttons on her coat were not lined up with the right openings, and her boots were on the wrong feet.

"Mom says you need to come inside. She has class in fifteen minutes, and she's going to be late. She doesn't want me in the house alone." Her bottom lip stuck out.

Cleo had stolen his heart the minute he laid eyes on her when his sister gave birth five years ago. Cleo was so much like Sloane. He would protect her at all costs as if she were his own.

He tossed a glance at Faith's door. She had said she didn't like Christmas. He couldn't imagine why, but who could turn down a sweet child excited about Santa and Christmas decorations? An idea popped into his head. He ruffled Chloe's hair.

"Let's go inside before your mom gets mad at me."

Cleo slid her tiny hand into his.

They might have a chance to win after all.

# CHAPTER 5

Faith opened her eyes for the hundredth time and gave up. The possibility of sleep burned off like morning fog. No one should be awake at this hour. The clock on the bedside table with its red numbers read 5:30 and laughed at her.

She threw her legs over the side of the bed, ignored the pain in her hip from either middle age or a bad mattress, and hobbled out of the room. The temperature in the house dropped during the night because the drafts snuck in under doors and around windows like a thief stealing heat from a radiator. Rubbing her arms, she put water on to boil and tossed logs in the fireplace.

Sleep had evaded her all night. Every time she closed her eyes, she either saw the Christmas card with its threatening message, or Zane in his black parka and his sheepish grin. She could never be with a man that into Christmas.

If she was going to be honest, she wasn't all that upset he had tried to string lights on her tree. She'd been secretly hoping he'd come knocking on her door again. Still, no romance would be in her future with him. He was bossy, and then there was the Christmas thing. Not to mention, she could never be completely honest. He appeared to be a man who didn't miss much. He would never miss the holes in her story about her past. Best to keep her distance. A relationship built on lies was bound to crumble like falling rubble.

She pulled down a mug from the cabinet and inspected it. Someday she would live in a house filled with objects that belonged to her and her alone. She wanted to stop running. She was tired of looking over her shoulder. She let out a long breath. Did she dare think about a family of her own?

The card had thrown her, and she had believed the police never came. That was why she had been rude while she talked to Zane. If she had realized one of those men on her lawn were him, she would've gone outside herself and told him to take the lights down. It would've been a good excuse to talk to him and not argue. He had been trying to apologize, and she hadn't made it easy. Maybe she could stop by with cookies or something just to be neighborly.

She needed to stop. He could have a fiancé or

something. A man that good-looking who played Santa for kids had to be taken by some lucky girl. Or guy.

Her phone vibrated against the kitchen counter. She jumped. It was too early for calls. If the Christmas card sender had found her number too, there would be no place to run away to.

She debated on answering, but her damn curiosity made her peek at the phone. The photo staring back at her allowed her to swipe the screen with relief. "Hey, Molly."

"Good morning, Sunshine. It's a beautiful day." Her agent's voice came through the phone full of saccharin-covered joy.

"You are far too perky this early in the morning. What are you doing up?" The tea kettle whistled the arrival of hot water. She might have to consider switching to coffee if she had more nights like last night.

"Who needs sleep? How's the book coming?" The clicking of keys at rapid speed echoed in the background.

"I'm working on it." If she only had half the energy Molly did, then maybe the book would be done.

"Will you make the new deadline?" Molly landed right on the point.

She had answered the phone hoping Molly would bring good news of an increase in sales or an offer for coffee like Zane had last night. His offer she had to turn down, but an afternoon with a friend would be a nice distraction.

"What if I can't make the deadline? Will they give me an extension?" She hated being the author who couldn't stick to her word.

She glanced over to the dining room table where the red envelope still sat. If whoever wrote that was really after her and had hunted down Faith Rudolph, she might not get a chance to finish the book at all.

"No extensions. Have you made a decision about revealing Mac Addison?"

"I still don't see why we have to do this."

"Here's the thing." The keyboard clicking stopped. "The publisher wants Mac on talk shows and social media live posts to interact with readers. Marketing is already setting up opportunities. You either get on board or you're out of your contract."

"Are you serious?"

"I'm sorry, Faith. I hate playing hardball with you. If you want to make the initial reveal on your own terms, they're fine with it. But either way, you're coming out."

She needed to keep her identity a secret until whoever was after her had been dealt with. She had no idea how to fix her problem. She didn't know who her parents were tangled up with. That was something they had kept from her. They thought they were protecting her from their life of crime, but they had failed at that because they were murdered on Christmas for something the killer never found. She suspected the item in question was jewelry because she'd figured out as a teenager her parents were thieves, but she didn't have what these people wanted.

She went over to the card and gripped it in her hand. "I need to get to the bottom of something first. Hold off the publisher for as long as you can." She ended the call.

So much for staying put in one place. It was time to go again. She flipped open her laptop and started searching for houses to rent right over the state line in Idaho. The options would be limited eleven days from Christmas, and she would waste time packing and driving again, but it had to be done. She could dictate the rest of the story in the car and then transcribe it later. She knew plenty of authors who did this for their whole novels. It wasn't a practice she encouraged, but it would work in an emergency, and this was one.

FAITH TOSSED her glasses on the table and rubbed her eyes. Her shoulders ached from the hours at the computer. All that effort, and not a decent rental anywhere. She found a few that would make her afraid to close her eyes at night and that didn't include the spooky card. She had enough to worry about without being concerned stray bullets from drive-bys would come through the window. The little Victorian on Gerald Avenue would have to do for now. Later she'd check other states.

The doorbell shattered the silence. She flinched but forced herself to go to the door. The lace curtain over the glass on the window revealed the silhouette of a small woman. Not likely anyone she should be worried about. Killers don't ring doorbells anyway.

She opened the door. "Can I help you?"

The woman turned her gaze from the street. Her smile broke across her wrinkled face. Her eyes still held the brightness of an active life reserved for younger people. "Hello. My name is Judy Beatrice. I live on the other side of the Cutlers. I wanted to welcome you to the neighborhood." Judy Beatrice handed over a round tin with the picture of a waving cartoon Santa on the lid.

The metal bottom was warm and soothed her cold fingers. "Thank you. It's nice to meet you. I'm Faith." A sense of relief washed over her skin as she stared at Judy. Maybe it was the emotional roller coaster she lived on, or maybe it was the nice gesture of a warm gift, but standing in front of Judy made her need a hug.

"There was also a card on your porch." Judy dropped a red envelope on the top of the tin.

The tin wobbled in her grip. The envelope was addressed to her again without a return address or a stamp.

"Oh, careful, dear. Those brownies just came out of the oven. The tin must be too hot to handle." Judy covered Faith's hands with her own.

"Does someone on the street hand-deliver cards?" She willed her heart to slow down.

"Well, sometimes Sue does. She has three little ones. Lives on the corner. I always mail mine. It's quicker to go to the post office than drive from house to house. That's probably from Sue."

If it was, how did she know her last name? A question she couldn't voice to her new neighbor. She hadn't told a soul her last name since she'd been here. "I'm sure it is. That's very thoughtful of her to include me."

"We have a slew of lovely neighbors. Everyone watches out for each other. It doesn't hurt that we have a professional bodyguard on the street either. We all feel a little safer because of Zane. Have you met him?"

So, Zane was a bodyguard. She wasn't surprised considering his size, and muscle mass. She didn't miss his pecs or his arms the first night he showed up on her porch. "We've met."

A loud ringing from Judy's coat cut her off before

the words could come out of her open mouth. She pulled a phone out of her pocket. "Oh, if you'll excuse me. It's my daughter. Merry Christmas. Enjoy the brownies." Judy waved as she hurried down the front steps.

Faith closed the door and placed the tin on the club chair in the living room. Her hands shook as she sliced the envelope open with a finger and managed to get a paper cut in the process. She let out a long breath and shimmied the card free.

The same beige background and Christmas tree drawing with the "A Christmas Wish for You" message on the front. She opened the card and stifled a scream.

"You can run, but you can't hide." Was written in the same script as the other card.

Her knees gave out, and she dropped onto the chair. All of her ideas of packing up and moving suddenly seemed ridiculous. If the killers found her here, they would track her down anywhere. They believed she had what they wanted, but she didn't.

It was time to take some action. If the killers were coming, she'd meet them halfway.

## CHAPTER 6

ZANE FINISHED ADDING LIGHTED candy canes along the bushes against the house. The yard looked great, if not a little crowded with its ten-foot snowmen. Sloane continued to roll her eyes at him, but Cleo loved it. And so did he. Decorating for Christmas was his way to unwind. Since he was on disability and pissed off he couldn't work, he needed the distraction.

He was neck and neck with Davis on the Face-book page. The traffic at night picked up too. As many cars stopped at his house to take pictures as they did at Davis's. Zane had a chance to win this thing. If only, he could get Faith to light up the damn house, then the street could win too.

"Shit." The female voice drifted across the lawn to him.

He came around one of the snowmen and found

Faith struggling with what looked like a camera and a drill. Her face was red. He laughed and went over.

"Do you need some help?"

"No, thank you." She kept her eyes on her task and grunted as she struggled to get the screw into the wood. With her hands above her head, her fleece jacket rode up enough to reveal some skin.

The view made his insides heat up. He wanted to run a hand over her side to see how she would respond to his touch. "Are you sure? I'm pretty good with a drill."

"I've got it. Don't you have some decorating to do?"

"Actually, my yard looks great for now. It's yours that needs a little attention. I could finish stringing those lights if you don't want me to help you hang that security camera."

She dropped her arms and finally met his gaze with a huff. "How did you know it was a security camera? The guy at the store assured me it would be discreet."

"It might be, but you aren't. Why are you installing security? This is a safe street."

"Call me paranoid."

"I might after you called the police on me the other night. Is someone bothering you?"

He could check into it for her, if she'd let him. He needed something else to do to pass the time besides all the decorating. He also wanted to know what was happening on his street. Since he was the closest thing to a police officer around here, he believed it was his responsibility to keep his neighbors safe.

"I wouldn't use the word bothering." She climbed down the ladder.

"Do you know who it is? If you can describe them, I can have Bud Lewis talk with them." Sometimes teenagers got out of hand. They drank at night on weekends and wandered around with no destination. The school was only a block away. If they tired of playing basketball drunk, they'd start walking.

"I'm hoping to catch someone in the act."

"The act of what? Are you being harassed? You should go to the police. Don't take care of it yourself. You'll end up hurt." Too many people thought they were capable of handling intruders and ended up dead instead.

"I'll take care of it, but thank you." She smiled at him for the first time. Her face lit up the way he suspected it would.

She made the heat simmering inside his veins rise in a rush. "What's going on? Is this what had you so upset the other night?"

"You ask a lot of questions."

"I've been accused of that before. Questions make me good at what I do."

"Judy Beatrice mentioned you were a professional bodyguard. Do people hire you directly, or do you work for a company?"

"Okay, now you have my curiosity piqued. You can't ask me that kind of question and not tell me what's up. I live right here with my sister and my niece. I have to keep them safe. Did someone try to break in?"

"No. Nothing like that." She glanced off. It was quick, but he didn't miss it.

She was lying.

One thing he couldn't tolerate was a liar. "Faith, I'm going to give you a piece of advice. If you have trouble at your door, then you'd better take care of it. We have families, older couples, and Judy who lives alone living here. I won't allow anything to happen to these people. They were here first."

She crossed her arms over her chest and gnawed on her bottom lip. He didn't want to spook her if she needed help. He might be able coax some answers from her if she was willing to trust him a little.

"Is it an ex-husband?" He took a step back and shoved his hands in his pockets.

"I've never been married. But it's not that simple."

"If you tell me what's going on, whatever has you scared might be an easier fix than you realize."

She kept at that lip. Her torturous work made her lip fuller and red and distracted him from getting to the bottom of her problem. Instead, he wanted to push her mouth open with his tongue and save her from drawing blood. He shook the thoughts away before he did something to get him slapped. She wasn't interested in him. She'd made that crystal clear.

"I might need a bodyguard." Her words came out on a swoosh of air.

"Why don't you come over to my house?" He needed to get the hell out of his coat before he passed out from heat exhaustion.

"I can't." She backed up.

"We can talk about what's happening to you, and I can give you some suggestions. I'm on disability so technically I can't work, but if you do need a bodyguard, my team is the best. I'll put you in touch with the right person." He held out a hand and waved her closer.

"You said your sister and your niece live with you. Is there anyone else living in the house?"

"Just us three. Sloane got divorced a year ago. She needed a place to crash for a while, but the arrangement works. She ended up staying. When I'm on assignment, I can be gone for weeks at a time. She and Cleo get the house to themselves. You're safe with me. I promise."

He waited again for her to respond because a woman like Faith needed the time and space to make a decision. Someone had wounded her badly. He wasn't ready to believe an ex didn't exist.

She looked back at her house then returned her gaze to him. "Okay. Just until it gets dark."

"I'll make sure to walk you back." He offered his elbow.

She took it.

ZANE'S muscular arm under her touch sent waves of warm tingles over her skin. Faith unzipped her fleece jacket. The smell of fresh air clung to his barn coat. She wanted to lean into him but forced a safe distance between them.

He led her around the house to the back. Even in the winter, with the landscaping hibernating until spring, the yard was meticulous. The boxwoods around the house were trimmed to perfection. The white paint on the house looked fresh. Almost every spot of his front yard was decorated for Christmas.

The decorations weren't cluttered or unorganized. White lights twirled around posts, doors, and windows. They also made lines on the roof above the porch. He told a story with the pieces on the lawn. Mannequins made up groupings of carolers. A life-like Santa on a sled pulled a reindeer. The evergreens were all covered in lights and ornaments. The tasteful, but extreme decorations reminded her of her child-hood. The frozen tundra around her heart shifted.

"This is a bad idea." She could not go inside this man's house. His dark eyes and warm smile had scattered her brain. It had been so long since anyone had been around to care about her, she forgot for a second she was running from killers and living a lie.

"Don't run off." He gripped her wrist. "I want to help you."

"Why?"

"Because it's what I do."

It was his job. He didn't have any attraction to her. That should make her shoulders drop away from her ears, but it didn't. He had shaken free her dormant libido, and she had secretly hoped he might find her attractive too. Since he didn't, sharing her secret shouldn't hurt like a busted knee cap.

She needed to trust him. She didn't have any other choice. The killers were coming, and if she was going to fight back, she couldn't do it alone. She should look at Zane as an unexpected Christmas gift. She stifled a groan.

"I panicked. I'm sorry."

He led her into the house through the back door. A woman with long hair as dark as Zane's and a little girl that matched colored in a Christmas coloring book at the kitchen table. The room was warm, and the smell of juicy beef and vegetables lingered in the air. The two ladies at the table looked up at the sound of approaching footsteps.

"Hey, this is our new neighbor Faith. Faith, my sister Sloane, and my favorite niece Cleo." Zane hung his coat by the door and reached for hers.

Cleo's face beamed a beacon of light into the room. Her dark eyes held wonder, and her cheeks still showed the adorable roundness of a preschooler.

"Uncle Zane, I'm your only niece." Cleo shook a crayon at him.

"Smart as a whip, that kid." Zane's face beamed too.

A gorgeous man who cared about other people and loved children. He was damn near perfect and off-limits.

"It's not much, but I have a stew cooking in the slow cooker. You're welcome to join us for dinner." Sloane arranged the coloring pages into a neat pile, and gathered the crayons into a plastic box.

"Thank you, but I won't be staying long." She threw her fleece over her arm instead of handing it to Zane.

"Cleo, go get cleaned up for dinner." Sloane kissed the top of her daughter's head.

Zane lifted the lid of the slower cooker and pulled a piece of beef out with his fingers. "Yum."

Sloane slapped his arm. "Don't put your hands in my stew. Sometimes I think you're still twelve. Do you have any siblings, Faith?"

"Me? No."

"Consider yourself lucky."

"Hey." Zane tried to pull Sloane against him, but she slipped from his grip and slapped him away with a dish towel. Brother and sister laughed in the same key.

The idea of having a real family formed a boulder in her throat. She blinked away tears that sprang without warning. The damn holidays always made her melancholy and lonely. She missed her parents most this time of year. She also resented them more around the holidays. If they had been like other parents, they wouldn't be dead.

"You know, I just remembered I had soup on the stove. I'd better run back before I burn the house down." She hurried out the back door and slipped where the snow had refrozen.

Her butt collided with the corner of the cement step and shot a pain up her spine. Her pride bruised in the process. She risked a look over her shoulder. Zane stood in the doorway with his lips twitching.

"Are you all right?" He reached out a hand.

She waved him off and wished reindeer would come and whisk her away. "I'm fine."

He trotted down the steps and helped her up. His strong hand gripped her wrist and tugged her close. Heat flushed her cheeks.

"You can't leave before telling me what has you so upset that you're hanging cameras and falling down steps."

The war between telling him and not waged in her head. There was something about this man that made her put her reservations to the side. Or maybe she was tired of hiding. Especially since her publisher wanted to expose Mac Addison. For once, it would be a relief to drop the shield and just be who she was without fear.

"It's going to sound crazy."

"Try me."

## CHAPTER 7

Zane had never been inside his neighbor's house. He took in the small Victorian with its cut-up floor plan. Each room stood alone with an archway between them. The living room turned left into the dining room which turned into the kitchen. Faith stood at the head of the dining room table and pointed at two envelopes.

"Those look like Christmas cards." He wasn't following. Christmas cards were hardly a reason to hang security cameras.

"They are. The cards themselves aren't the problem. It's the message inside. Can I get you some coffee or a beer?"

"No, thanks. What does the message say?"

She flopped into the chair. At least she didn't go running out the back door again. "Someone thinks I have something that belongs to them."

"Do you have it?" He rubbed the ache in his shoulder.

The best way to solve this problem was to determine right up front if she was in possession of this object. The cards probably were from an ex who wanted his golf clubs back, and she was holding them hostage for more money. He still didn't believe there wasn't a man in her past worth mentioning.

"I don't know what they want."

"But you know who the cards are from?" He pulled out the seat opposite her and sat.

"Not exactly." She worked her lip under her teeth.

She would chew off a few layers if she continued. His gaze remained focused on her lips, but his mind wandered to what her lips would taste like if he could indulge in that assignment.

"Why do they think you have it?" His words caught on his dry throat. "You know what, I'd love that coffee if you're still offering."

She moved around in the kitchen, opening and closing cabinets. The single-cup coffee maker came to life with its gurgle and hiss. "I think it has to do with my parents."

"Have you told them about the cards?"

"They passed away when I was in college." She placed a mug and a tin of brownies in front of him.

"I'm sorry."

"Thanks."

"Pull out the cards so I can read the notes. I don't

want to pick them up if we need to try and grab prints off them. My prints will only make things worse."

She did as he asked and left them open on the table for him to read.

"Are you hiding?"

The color drained from her face. "Sort of."

"You either are or you aren't. You'd better start from the beginning and tell me everything." He wasn't sure what he was about to go up against, but he couldn't help her if he didn't know the whole story. Keeping her safe meant keeping his family and his street safe too.

"I really need to get that camera installed. Whoever left these walked right up to my porch. I need to see who it might be." She stood and tugged at the scarf around her neck.

"I have the resources to help you, but you can't continue to avoid the problem."

"You can help me by standing on a ladder and working the drill. My story won't stop them from coming back. They've been here twice." She blinked several times. A single tear escaped the corner of her eye. She pressed her palm to her face.

"If these are professionals, they will avoid your home security system without breaking a sweat. Stop holding back. You said you'd tell me." He should march right out of here and go home. She didn't want his help.

"Can I tell you while we hang the camera? Even if it's pointless, it will make me feel better having it."

"I'll hang the camera." The pain in her eyes thwarted his quest for information. He grabbed her hand and laced their fingers together.

She squeezed his hand. "Thank you."

The space between them hummed with a low current. She stared up at him with expectant eyes. Her tongue darted out onto her swollen lip. He leaned in, hoping that was an invitation.

A noise on the front porch broke the current. She stepped back.

"What was that?" she said.

"Stay here." He handed her his phone. "Don't hesitate to call for help."

He wished he had his gun. He turned out the lights in the front room before checking out the windows and the door. As far as he could tell, nothing looked out of the ordinary. He opened the door to a stiff Montana wind.

She was fast on his heels and leaned around him to see out the door. A red envelope waited on the welcome mat. She sucked in a breath.

"Go back inside. I'll take a look around. Lock the door behind me. Stay away from the windows." He took back his phone and closed the door.

He operated the flashlight app on his phone and walked her yard. The sun had set while they were inside. The front showed nothing but the bare branches blowing in the wind. The rest of the street appeared tucked in with cars in driveways and windows glowing with warm light. His own house seemed undisturbed too. Only the bright Christmas lights and decorations were the wake-up call. An intruder wouldn't be able to hide in his yard. He circled her house, but nothing seemed out of sorts. Whoever dropped the card and ran was fast and quiet. He knocked on the door. "Faith, it's me. Open up."

She stood in the doorway rubbing her arms. "Did you see anyone?"

"Nothing. I'm sorry. May I?" He pointed to the card.

"Go ahead."

He picked it up by its corner. It was a regular card bought at any card or grocery store. The envelope wasn't sealed. Smart. No DNA from saliva. He could take a guess then whoever left it knew not to leave prints. He eased the card out. As he suspected, a standard card with a typical picture. The inside had him a little concerned.

"You have nine days until the end." Was written in black ink.

"Nine days till the end of what?" He held the card for her to see.

"I don't know."

"It's nine days till Christmas. Is that significant?"

"Other than the fact Christmas is a huge holiday

and everyone is running around like crazy people buying up gifts they can't afford and decorating their lawns with enough lights to be seen from the moon?"

"You really do hate Christmas, don't you?"

"I just don't see the point. It's never brought me any joy."

"Then you haven't spent it with the right people." He would like the opportunity to show her how to enjoy the holiday if she'd let him. But those arms wrapped around her middle like a choke hold screamed stay away. The connection between them only minutes before was long forgotten. But not for him.

"This is serious, Zane. If I had the time, I'd move again, but I'm on this deadline, and I can't find another place suitable enough in such short notice. Can you please hang the camera? I don't want to stand here with the door wide open any longer. They could be watching."

"How about if I hang the camera and spend the night?" He closed the door.

"Excuse me?" Her eyes grew wide.

"Relax. It's not a come on. You're clearly upset. The camera won't be enough to ease your worry. I can keep a watch during the night. Make sure the camera works right."

"You'd have to move in to ease my mind. And that's not happening."

"You could hire me."

She laughed. "You said you're on disability. Plus, hiring a bodyguard is silly. That's for celebrities and politicians."

"Anyone can hire a bodyguard who doesn't feel safe. I'll put a call into my boss and tell him I'm doing a private job. He won't mind. What do you say?"

"How much do you charge?"

"Consider it a Christmas present."

# CHAPTER 8

FAITH TRIED TO WORK, but the words wouldn't come. All she could think about was the hot guy in her living room. He had made dinner after he hung up the camera and made sure it worked properly. Of course, he could cook. Why couldn't she have moved in next door to an old spinster with arthritis who liked to knit and had fifteen cats?

The memory of their almost kiss lingered in her mind like a good love story. She shoved out of the chair and paced the loft, hoping some idea for the book would come. She'd written so many romance novels she was burnt out. She didn't really know what love was anyway. She had been on the run for so long she never settled down with a guy long enough to actually fall. Besides, who would want to be in a relationship with someone who kept secrets from them? She had to keep her true identity hidden. Or maybe now that she had been discovered, she could tell the truth? Would that save her life?

She crept down the stairs not wanting to wake him if he had fallen asleep. The blue light of the television flickered in the living room, but the sound was low. The layout of the house allowed her to enter the kitchen through the dining room as well as the living room. If he was awake, he'd hear her. She wouldn't be able to hide from him. But if he was asleep, she could sneak back upstairs with her warm milk, and if she couldn't write maybe she could sleep.

She turned on the small light under the microwave then poured milk into a pot and reached for a large metal spoon to stir. The spoon slipped from her hand and clanked against the pot before clattering on the ground of her tiled floor.

"Are you okay?" Zane appeared in the doorway. His hair was disheveled on the side as if he'd been lying on it. His voice was laced with sleep.

"I'm sorry I woke you."

"I was just resting my eyes. Did you hear something outside?"

"I was trying to work but couldn't. I thought I'd get something to help me focus or sleep. Would you like some?" She held up the milk carton.

"No, thanks. I don't drink milk. I'll take a look around outside one more time."

"Wait." She didn't want to be alone, but the idea of telling him how afraid she was managed to burn her cheeks and silence her tongue.

"What's up?"

"I, um, do you think it's a good idea? What if they're watching?"

"At least they'll know you aren't alone any longer. Maybe they'll rethink whatever they're trying to do if they're worried about interference. So far, you haven't given them any reason to worry."

"I couldn't call the police. How would I explain myself and those cards?"

"You would start with the truth. How about you tell me that story now, since you can't sleep?" He leaned against the wall and waited.

Did her parents' career really matter if they were dead? She poured the warm milk into a mug. She went into the sunroom where there was a table and hoped he'd follow.

He did without question. She didn't need the milk to warm her insides while he was around.

"Can I ask you a question first?" She eyed him over the top of her mug.

He took the seat opposite her. The room was dark except for the glow of the snow-covered ground spilling through the large windows that looked out onto the backyard. When she first got here, she didn't like those windows with all their visibility, but with

Zane, she wasn't as worried. He wouldn't let anything happen.

"The lady has a question. Okay, one question in exchange for your story."

"Why do you like Christmas so much?"

"What's there not to like about Christmas?" He ran a hand through his hair and smoothed down the ones in the back.

"Where do you want me to start? The gifts? The fake charities scamming money. The cookies. The cheesy movies. The just as cheesy decorations." She fixed him her knowing gaze. She used to love decorating the house with her parents when she was little. But then she learned about their method of employment right around the time the teen years kicked in.

"Okay. I get your point. You sound like Scrooge." A smile laced his words.

"A Christmas Carol should be considered a tragedy." She snuggled into the chair and let out a long breath. The milk or the company eased the discomfort in her belly.

He sputtered out a laugh. "That's my favorite book. I read it every year."

"Of course, you do."

"I'm going to change your perspective on Christmas." He wagged a finger at her.

"I doubt that." She wondered what he had in mind and almost asked, but didn't. Allowing him to thaw the ice around her holiday heart was dangerous. She survived by freezing out Christmas and any emotion that resembled caring for someone else.

"Will you let me try?"

"You really seem to enjoy a challenge." The mug was empty. She got up to pour more. He was fast on her heels with his confident stride. A tingle ran over her skin. She'd been celibate too long.

"Come with me tomorrow. I'm picking out our Christmas tree. You could get one too."

She remembered all the Christmases as a child with her parents. The three of them used to cut down their tree every year. Her father would always let her pick the tree she wanted. The bigger the better. She hadn't had a tree since they died. The idea of putting one up and decorating it when they were both killed in front of theirs was too much to handle. That tree had brought so much joy and more pain than she could bear most days.

"I don't know. I have a lot of work to do." She had been avoiding Molly's calls. When she finished the book, she would hand it in and say goodbye to Mac Addison. She just wasn't sure how yet.

"We'll only be a couple of hours. You can work right up until we leave and when we get back. I won't ask you to come over and help us decorate."

This could be her last Christmas if the sender of the cards meant business. That thought sent another shiver over her skin, and not a warm and fuzzy kind. The idea of being alone in the house turned the milk sour in her stomach. "Would I be safe out in the open like that?"

"You're safe with me. Don't worry."

She had a feeling her fears would subside around him. She shouldn't like that thought so much.

But she did.

# CHAPTER 9

ZANE CHECKED the security camera footage for the few hours he dozed at Faith's house. He didn't think he'd fall asleep after Faith came downstairs in her fleece pajama pants and tight-fitting top. The sight of her had him thinking about what her skin under that shirt would taste like. He had tried to keep his gaze glued to her eyes while he convinced her to come tree shopping, but that black shirt hugged her in all the right places. She was beautiful, and he wasn't dead. Now he had a date. Okay, not a real date.

He clicked through the footage on his laptop and sipped coffee in his kitchen. The sunrise washed the black out of the sky like ink from a shirt. Not one thing came near Faith's porch all night. He'd left there only a half hour ago for a quick shower. He needed to wash the sleep out of his brain and cool his hormones a little. She was making his body sit up and take notice of things he hadn't noticed in a while. He had sworn off women, and she was making him reconsider that for a minute or two or twenty.

There was a good chance whoever was leaving the cards knew about the camera. If they were determined, they'd just leave the card somewhere else. Or worse. He would install cameras at the back of the house after they went tree shopping. If she'd allow it, he would also spend the night on the couch again. He wanted to be there if the unsub returned. And selfishly, he wanted to see her in those pajamas again.

He poured more coffee and took a big inhale of the earthy scent. The fog in his brain pushed back a little. The cards were a tactic to scare the hell out of her. It appeared to be working, but she held it together well. He'd seen people fall apart over a lot less. He hoped these card people weren't prepared to kill her for whatever they wanted, but he'd need to be prepared. That meant a call to his boss.

He searched Hank's number, hit the call button, and waited for Hank to answer.

"Patterson."

"It's Cutler."

"Cutler. How's vacation?"

"Not much of a vacation, sir. It's winter in Montana." And the light contest. He can't slack off there no matter how much he wanted to help Faith.

"I hope you're taking it easy. That's an order."

"Trying." He wasn't trying too hard, which his boss would find out soon enough.

"How's the shoulder?"

"Fine." It hurt every morning when he woke up. The cold got right inside his bones and made the ache turn up fifty notches. He still couldn't raise his arm completely over his head without gritting his teeth. None of which Hank Patterson needed to know.

"Okay, Cutler. Get to it. Why the call?"

"I'm taking a pro bono job while I'm recuperating."

"As long as you aren't getting paid, I can't stop you from being charitable, and I don't like turning people away who need help. But it's going on the record that I don't like the idea of you working while you're hurt."

"I thought you might say that."

"Then why mention it?"

"Because that's our deal." He followed orders, mostly. He hadn't been following orders when he was injured in the army and had to retire. The guilt gave him nightmares.

"Who are you helping?"

"I'm helping someone who can't help themselves, and I'm doing it with honor. Indirectly, you're helping too."

"You're blowing smoke up my ass. Let me ask one more time." Hank waited for his answer.

"I'm helping my neighbor." He was also interested in getting to know his neighbor better, but he'd leave that part out.

"Name?"

"Faith."

"She just goes by Faith? Like Cher or Madonna?"

He scratched the back of his neck and braced himself for what was about to come at him. "I don't know her last name."

"Please tell me you are joking." Hank groaned.

"No, sir." He expected Hank to yell. Maybe Christmas just came early.

"I should fire you."

"But you won't." He hoped.

"Only because I know you will have that last name by the end of the hour. Am I clear?"

"Yes, sir." Relief pushed the corners of his mouth into a smile. He would make sure to ask Faith all the right questions.

"If you hurt that shoulder worse, you're getting demoted. I appreciate all my men and women and their strong work ethic, but you are all also a pain in my ass when it comes to admitting you're hurt. Everyone knows you're tough, but you're human. That wasn't a sprain. It was a tear which you didn't disclose."

"Linc ratted me out." He didn't blame Lincoln. He was the lead on the team. The pain hurt like a bitch, and Linc caught him favoring his arm. No one lied to Linc and lived to talk about it.

"What's this pro bono work that my better judgment tells me to stay out of?"

He filled Hank in on what he knew. "I don't know where to start. I've never seen threats like these."

"You might have a starting point if you knew her last name."

Heat flushed his face. "I did search murders that happened on Christmas in the last twenty years. She revealed that much without realizing she did. I can't find anything that points to the murder of a husband and wife survived by one daughter. Do you have any ideas?"

Her disdain for Christmas and the death of her parents sent him on the chase for a murder around Christmastime. He hoped she would tell him the details and make his job easier. Unless she had something to hide.

"You're sure the people leaving the cards are the same ones who killed her parents?"

"She is."

"You're going to see more cards then. Count on it. As far as digging into her past, ask her. If she hides important intel from you, then bounce her. You can't protect someone who lies. She'll only manage to get you into trouble you can't get out of."

"If she won't tell me everything, then she's

involved." He didn't want to say that out loud, but Hank had to be thinking it. They were trained for this kind of thing. Anyone who was guilty had something to hide. If she didn't, she'd spill just to make the fear stop.

"Most likely. If she doesn't want to spill on who the murderers were, they are most likely formidable. You shouldn't be on this alone."

"I can handle it."

"Your team isn't on assignment. You can have Smith, Montero, and Porter if you need them. I'll pay them."

"You just said you were against me doing this."

"Yeah, well, if Montero doesn't have a job soon, he'll drive everyone around here crazy with all the baby pictures." Hank laughed.

"Thanks. I'll let you know if I get stuck."

"Let me know before you get stuck. Good luck." Hank ended the call.

Zane rinsed the mug and deposited it in the dishwasher. Deep red streaks intersected a whitewashed sky. The trees swayed in the morning breeze. He grabbed his coat and went out the back. He wanted to catch his neighbor as she was waking up. If he wasn't already too late. He had a question to ask her. And he wanted to see those pajamas again.

## CHAPTER 10

FAITH CHECKED every room in the house. She let out a long breath. No sign of Zane other than the folded blanket at the end of the couch. He hadn't so much as left a note. Not much of a bodyguard if he left her all alone after she told him she didn't want to be alone. That was the only reason why she had agreed to go buy a dumb Christmas tree. Okay, not the only reason.

Maybe he didn't really believe her. It didn't matter. They were coming for her. If the last card was right, in nine days. Eight now. Christmas Day. She had better figure out what the hell they wanted by then, or she'd end up like her parents.

A knock on the door sent her two feet off the floor. Her heart hammered her ribs. "Pull it together. Murderers don't knock."

She opened the door to Zane on her front porch.

Her gaze dropped to the ground. Nothing on the mat. His hands were shoved in his pockets. No card there either.

"Why did you leave?"

"What's your last name?" He pushed past her into the living room.

"I didn't invite you in." She followed fast on his heels, knowing full well she wouldn't throw him out now that he had returned. But he didn't need to know that exactly.

"Of course, you did. The second you hired me to protect you."

"I haven't paid you. Therefore, I haven't bought a thing. You can go. I don't need your services. You aren't very good at your job." She kept her distance from him because if she didn't, she would try to recreate their moment in the sunroom last night.

He unzipped his jacket and tossed it on the couch. His black-and-red flannel hung untucked from his jeans. The top buttons were opened and exposed the spot of skin between his collarbones. She bet if she touched him there his skin would be soft. The sleeves of the flannel were rolled up to reveal a white long-sleeved shirt underneath. A flash of heat ran over her body. She wanted to blame it on a hot flash.

"What is it you don't like about me, Faith?"

She liked everything about him. That was the problem. "You left the house without informing me. What if someone delivered another card or broke in?

How can you protect me if you aren't here?" Her voice climbed the stairs of panic. She tried to force it back down but only managed to stand on her toes instead.

He smiled and shook his head. "You were sound asleep when I left. I wasn't going to wake you because you had so much trouble sleeping."

"But you —"

"Hang on. I was gone a total of forty-five minutes. Before I left, I made sure all the doors and windows were locked. I checked the entire perimeter of the house. The software for the security camera will send a notice to my phone if someone moves near it. Considering the two cards you've received so far were delivered in the middle of the night, I figured a six-thirty shower was okay. My gun was never more than a foot away from me." He lifted his shirt. A mean-looking black gun was attached to his hip.

"Okay. I guess." She wasn't ready to concede even if he did prove his point. She had a right to be a nervous wreck.

"I'm good at my job. You don't have to worry, but I can't do my job if you don't tell me everything I need to know."

"What else do you need to know?"

"Let's start with a last name."

"I haven't told you my last name?" She tried to run her mind over their conversations, but the ridges in her memory were too smooth to catch.

The image of him sitting with her last night in the shadows of the sunroom blocked all her other thoughts. What did he look like without that shirt on? The living room seemed to close in on her. She went into the kitchen. He followed.

"No, ma'am. No last name, birth date, or blood type." He flashed his bright smile. She could forgive him for calling her ma'am if he continued to look at her like he wanted to know her deepest thoughts.

"It's Rudolph." She needed to keep busy and grabbed mugs out of the cabinet. She held one up.

"I've had mine, but thanks. What else can you tell me about yourself?" He leaned against the counter and crossed his ankles.

She had lost her way with all the running she'd been doing. Maybe she could find a way home and share just a little of herself for once.

"My parents were murdered on Christmas. Shot in the head and propped up in front of the tree. I found them." Saying the words hurt less than she expected.

"I'm so sorry. That must've been very hard for you."

"I'd say." She fumbled with the tea bags. Several spilled on the floor.

"Do you know why someone wanted your parents dead?" He ushered her back, retrieved them, and started making the tea.

"I didn't stick around to find out what the police

learned. As soon as I was cleared of any involvement, I packed up what would fit in my car and drove until I couldn't anymore. I landed in Indiana. It seemed like a quiet enough place. So I stayed for a while."

"The police never figured out who killed them?"

"I'm pretty sure that was the killer's plan."

"I will dig into whoever is leaving those cards. No one should go through what you have." He placed a mug of hot water on the counter beside her.

"Can't we just stop them in the act?" That would be so much easier.

"I'm hoping to do that. Then I can ask them directly what the hell is going on. But if they don't leave any more cards, or until they do, I want to find out who I'm dealing with. I might be able to figure out what their end game is before they act on it."

She swallowed the lump blocking her airway. The end game would be the end of her because she didn't know what they wanted. Her parents never discussed the details of their business with her.

"But the messages are threatening. Isn't that a crime?"

"They haven't said anything about hurting you. And even if they did, we need to know who they might be at least. If it's who murdered your parents, then that's the place to start."

She couldn't imagine it was anyone else. They had found her while in Indiana. She had fled to New

Mexico after that then back up to Montana where she thought she'd lost them.

"Okay, Faith Rudolph, that's enough for now. I've got a solid place to start. Today is for cutting down Christmas trees and drinking hot cocoa. After that, I will let you get to work like promised."

She hesitated. Her brain warred with her heart. She should stay at home, behind locked doors, and work. Or she could let this man show her a good time for a few hours. It might even help her get past the creative block she'd bumped into.

"Are you changing your mind about coming?" He dipped his head and fastened a knowing gaze on her.

"No." Maybe. That smile of his made something low in her belly tingle. She grabbed her coat and on unsteady legs locked the door, glanced at the camera, and followed Zane.

"My TREAT." Faith held up a slender hand. "You were nice enough to bring me along today, the least I can do is buy you and Cleo a hot chocolate."

Zane pushed his wallet back into the front pocket of his jeans and tried to ignore the way his chest puffed up around this woman. She hadn't blinked when he announced Cleo had to come along at the last minute. Sloane had to go out and couldn't take her. Faith and Cleo had held hands and ran around the tree lot trying to decide on the perfect tree. Now she was insisting on contributing by picking up the cocoa.

He squatted down and handed Cleo a hot chocolate. Her brown eyes had grown to the width of a tree trunk. His heart warmed. "Blow on it. You don't want to burn your mouth, okay?"

The Christmas tree farm burst with people choosing trees and drinking hot cocoa. Families made memories surrounded by the scent of balsam and cedar. When he and Sloane were kids, their parents took them out every year to pick a tree and cut it down. Their dad wouldn't let anyone but him cut the tree. They'd drag it back, and Dad would tie it to the car with unwanted directions from his mother. The first time his dad let him help—he had to be around Cleo's age—a branch from the tree fell off. He had kept that branch in a pot for months. Even long after the needles had fallen off and been swept away.

His niece wrapped her small hands around the Styrofoam cup. She scrunched her shoulders up by her ears, and pushed out a big puff of air. The spiral of whipped cream broke into small wet clouds that landed on his face. He blinked twice and laughed.

"I'm sorry." Cleo wiped his face with her free hand.

"It's no big deal." Sticky maybe. He stood tall and licked the cream off his top lip. Warm and sweet. The way he imagined Faith would taste. The thought knocked him off-balance. Having an attraction to his neighbor could lead to trouble. He knew better than to get involved with a client. He had enough trouble of his own to carry around.

Faith handed him a napkin. "It's a good look for you." Her lips twitched as if she tried to force the smile into neutral, but the sparkle in her eyes gave away her pleasure.

"Do I amuse you?" The thought of his tongue on her skin shoved its way back. Getting involved with a client wasn't any more appropriate than his errant thoughts with his niece around.

"You look a little like Santa. Cleo, don't you agree?" She dabbed his chin with another napkin.

Cleo giggled. What was left of the whipped cream was now around Cleo's mouth. Sloane might not be happy about the amount of sugar they had consumed.

He grabbed Faith's hand and met her gaze because if she went on touching him like that, he might kiss her on the spot. "Let's hit the road. We have a tree to put up and Miss Faith has to get back to work."

"You're not going to help us decorate it?" Cleo's mouth drooped. The wonder in her eyes disappeared like melted snow.

"I would love to, but I do have some work to do. Maybe if it's not too much trouble, you could save one ornament for me to hang?" She adjusted Cleo's hat and fastened a high-voltage smile on her.

His stomach flipped and landed on its head. He wanted to know why a woman that was so great with kids didn't have any. She couldn't have the same kind of broken past he had when it came to love. Any man would be lucky to have her.

"Uncle Zane, you're not listening." Cleo tugged on the bottom of his coat.

"I'm sorry. What did you say?" Because he was too busy getting lost in thoughts of Faith and not paying any attention to what they were talking about.

"Can we save one ornament for Miss Faith to hang? Please?"

"Yeah, sure. Let's go. Your mom is going to wonder where we are." The sun was starting to set, and the wind picked up speed. The air smelled like snow. He didn't want Sloane to worry. She had probably checked the family location app about a hundred times.

Cleo took his hand in one of hers and Faith's in the other. Faith smiled at him over Cleo's head. She ducked her head, and her hair fell over her face. They were the picture of a real family. His breath stuck in his throat.

"Hey, Zane. Is that you? Wait up." A familiar voice drifted across the parking area toward them.

He stifled a groan. Maria Emerson dodged parked cars on a mission toward him. The woman was like a mosquito at dusk. "Hello, Maria. Getting a tree?" What else would she be doing here, but he had to say something.

"George and the kids are tying it to the car about now. I saw you and had to run over. Hello, Cleo, dear."

Cleo ducked behind his leg.

"Anyway." Maria's hand swatted at the air. "How are the decorations coming? Our entire street is lit. I'm so excited. Everyone participated and not just with lights. Everyone has a display from the Twelve Days of Christmas. Since we have twelve houses, everyone took a day. Have you seen the Facebook page? We're in the lead." She clapped her hands and squealed.

He wanted to take a step back, but Cleo and the bumper of a car were right behind him. He hadn't seen the page today. As of a couple of days ago, the street was holding its own. Maria's street wasn't even on the radar yet. She must've banged on every door day and night or simply put the decorations up herself. He stole a quick glance at his non-competing neighbor. He couldn't get mad at her, but he still wanted to win.

"Don't take this the wrong way, Maria, but you won't have the lead for long. Our street always wins." His words fell flat even to him. He wouldn't let her get the best of him in front of Cleo and Faith. He gritted his teeth and held Maria's gaze.

"Oh, not this year. You should really check the page. We're ahead by a lot. I drove down your street. Your new neighbor isn't participating. The old neighbors, what were their names, oh yeah, the Barrys at least threw a few lights on. You'll never catch up if this new neighbor doesn't put up something, and just a few lights won't do it. You and Davis can't carry the street anymore. My street has finally done a fantastic job, and I couldn't be prouder of us." She took a quick breath. "I'm sorry, we weren't introduced. I'm Maria Emerson." Maria stuck out her hand toward Faith.

Faith gave a quick shake, but instead of putting her hand back down at her side, she looped her hand around his arm instead. "I'm Faith. The new neighbor you mentioned. I wouldn't count Gerald Avenue out just yet. I admit I haven't had a chance to put up my decorations with the new move and all, but they'll be up in time for the final vote. I wouldn't let Zane and the others down."

He hoped his jaw wasn't at his boots. His arm seemed to have caught fire, but he was okay with that. "I guess we'll have to see how the competition plays out," he said.

Maria scrunched up her face and shook her head. "We're still ahead. You're going to have to campaign for more votes to win. I'd better get going." She hurried off between the cars without waiting for a response.

"Thanks for saying that even if it wasn't true.

She's a real pain in the butt. Brags about everything. I don't know how her husband stands it. You shut her up for a second. I've never been able to do that."

"Uncle Zane, you said shut up." Cleo gave him the stern look she learned from Sloane.

"Sorry. Don't tell your mom."

Faith had come to his rescue and defended their street. He pulled her into him without thinking. Her hair smelled like flowers. She leaned against his chest for a second but pulled away.

"Your jaw was clenched. I thought you might break a tooth. Plus, she was braggy. I meant what I said. I don't want you to lose to her. If the offer still stands, could you help me put up some decorations on the lawn?"

"You bet. I have a whole bunch in my basement. I have a few ideas if you aren't opposed."

"Whatever you think is best. Maybe tomorrow? I do have to get work done today, and I need to check the mail." She arched an eyebrow.

"I'll help you do both." He picked up Cleo and spun her around. "Okay, squirt, tomorrow we're taking the competition by storm. You ready to help?"

Cleo's giggles and squeals made his heart soar. "Yes."

He ushered them back to his truck where the tree was tied to the roof. They had picked a good one this year. He slid his hand through Faith's. She didn't back away or shove her hand in her pocket. Instead, she gave him a hint of a smile.

She stopped short and sucked in a breath. He tried to see what she was looking at when his gaze landed on the spot.

Tucked under the windshield wiper of his truck was a red envelope.

# CHAPTER 11

FAITH COULDN'T BREATHE. The sounds of people laughing and talking about trees and holidays and good cheer drifted away. Her head was full and heavy as if she were on an airplane getting ready to land. The killers had followed them.

Zane pushed her and Cleo against a car. "Get down. Stay here until I say so."

"What's the matter?" Cleo's voice trembled.

She gathered the little girl in her arms and hunkered down in front of the tire. "It's okay, sweetie. Uncle Zane wants to check on something." She prayed her own voice didn't betray her. Could she convince the girl this was nothing more than a game that adults liked to play? She needed to stay strong for Cleo, but the killers could be anywhere. It would be all her fault if something happened to Zane and his family. Another family couldn't suffer because of her parents and their tainted past.

Zane hurried toward the truck with his hand on his hip where he had shown her the gun. She couldn't see what he was doing, but had to trust him. He was her only hope now.

"I want to stand up." Cleo squirmed in her arms.

"Not yet, sweetie. We're playing a game of hide and seek. We have to hide until Uncle Zane finds us."

"But he put us here. That's not how hide and seek works."

The logic of a five-year-old made her laugh. "This is a different kind of game. We hide, and he runs off in the maze of cars. He has to remember where he put us before we count to a hundred. Can you count to a hundred?" She had no idea if she was making any sense. She only hoped she could distract Cleo enough.

"I can. One, two, three…" Cleo continued to count.

She prayed.

Somewhere around Cleo counting to twenty, Zane returned out of breath. "It's okay. Come on." He helped them up and swung Cleo in his arms.

"Are you sure?" She held onto the back of his jacket to keep up.

"Yes." His voice was clipped. This wasn't the same man who just picked a tree with his niece. He was either mad at her for bringing trouble to his doorstep, or he had become a man with liquid steel in his veins and a job to do.

With everyone in the truck, he backed out and headed home. He didn't mention the card or anything else the whole way. Neither did she. Talking about this in front of Cleo would only scare her, and Faith didn't want that to happen.

The front end of the truck dipped in his driveway as he took the turn on two wheels. They shook in their seats. Her teeth rattled around in her head. He threw the truck in park with force and helped Cleo unbuckle her seatbelt. "Stay by my side while I get Cleo inside."

"But Uncle Zane, the tree. We have to set it up."

"We will, sweetie. But first, I have to do a job for Miss Faith."

"What kind of job?" Cleo rubbed her eyes.

"I need to look inside her house. She lost something." Zane looked over his shoulder. His gaze raked the street.

Did he see something? Because she couldn't. Anyone could be lurking around a bush or hidden in the glow of a brightly lit, oversized, inflatable decoration.

"What did you lose?" Cleo rested her head on Zane's shoulder as he unlocked the back door.

"Oh, um…I…" Her mind raced to find a suitable thing to lie about but came up empty.

"It's a grown-up thing. I'll tell you when you're big." He pushed open the door.

The warmth from the kitchen spilled across them. She shivered in her coat. Sloane turned from the stove. Her smile fell off her face when she saw them. The woman knew her brother well and recognized the cold stare in his otherwise warm eyes.

"Is everything okay?" Sloane's gaze bounced between her and Zane.

"Has anyone been around today?" He handed Cleo to Sloane and ignored her question.

"No. Why?" She raised an eyebrow.

"Lock the doors behind me. Don't come outside until I come back."

"Zane, tell me what's up."

"Not now, Sloane. Do as I say." The terse words made Sloane jump back. She clutched harder to Cleo.

Faith flinched too.

"Let's go." He grabbed her wrist and pulled her outside.

The cold wind shoved its way under her coat. She would never be warm again. If she hurt this family, she would deserve that and more. She had allowed a small attraction to risk too much.

"Zane, I'm sorry—"

"Let me check your house first. We can talk after. Give me your house keys."

She fumbled in her purse until she found them.

"Stay on the porch."

He unlocked the front door and put a finger to his lips to silence any ideas she might have of asking questions. She nodded her understanding, but the pounding of her heart would certainly give them away.

He removed his gun from the holster and went inside. Lights popped on in each room. The glow throughout the house did nothing to ease her worry until he stepped back on the porch holstering his gun.

"Pack a bag." He shoved his hands on his hips. The determined glare remained in his eyes.

"Excuse me?"

"You aren't staying here tonight, and I can't be in two places at once. I need to make sure Sloane and Cleo are safe since your trouble is now at my front door too." He ran a hand over his face. "That's on me, but I have a family to protect. Everyone under the same roof. I'm going to need to call backup."

"Not the police."

"Why not?"

"I don't trust them."

"You don't know them."

"I know officers like them. When you hear my story, you'll understand why I need to go outside the conventional police force."

"Well, lucky for you I have those resources."

"Thank you."

"Don't thank me. I'm mad as hell that Sloane and

Cleo are involved. I should throw you to the wolves and let you take care of yourself, but that's anger talking. You're in trouble, and I'll help you because that's what I'm trained to do. Now pack a bag. I want to get back."

"Did you open the card?"

He wiggled the card free from his coat pocket and handed it to her. With shaking hands, she tore the card out. "Give us what we want or we'll take something of yours." She turned the card for Zane to see.

"What do they want, Faith?"

"I don't know."

"That better be the truth."

It was most of it.

## CHAPTER 12

FAITH DROPPED her bag beside the daybed in the room adjacent to Zane's. The rooms shared a door as if at one time this room may have been a nursery or office. The only way into the hallway was through Zane's room.

A small wood desk faced the wall. The top was covered in papers, a laptop, and a homemade pencil holder decorated in the handwriting of a five-year-old. She didn't need to read the *love Cleo* part to guess where it came from.

She pushed out a long breath and paced the small space. The one window looked out onto the back-yard that was nothing more than shadows and dark corners. Zane had asked her to wait here while he explained what happened to Sloane. Her presence was not wanted while he discussed the trouble she brought on the people he loved most.

Her laptop waited to be opened and used. She couldn't begin to write after what happened today. She would never make the Christmas Eve deadline. She would have to call Molly and tell her. She would also be telling her there was no way on this planet Mac Addison would surface. They could tell the world he died and the last book would never be published. She grabbed her phone and dialed.

"Please tell me this is one of your sick jokes?" Sloane slapped her thigh.

"Keep your voice down. I don't want Cleo or Faith to hear us." Zane took a quick look up the steps to the second floor. The stairway was empty.

"I don't care about your new friend. I care about my daughter's safety. Never, in all the years you've worked for the Brotherhood has danger come to our doorstep. If I had thought for a second what you did for a living would put Cleo in harm's way, I would never have agreed to live here."

"Come on. You're being melodramatic. What I do is no different than what a police detective or an FBI agent does. They have families."

"You don't investigate. You protect. That's different." She scooped her hair off her face. Dark circles hung like half-moons under her eyes.

"I can't let her go without help." He would never leave someone behind who needed help.

"Get her someone else to watch over her. Hank must have a hundred men and women working for him."

He opened his mouth to respond, but he clamped it shut. It would be simple to call Hank and have him bring a car around for Faith. Any one of the guys could keep an eye on her. They could even bunk at her house, but the idea of anyone else keeping watch instead of him made the underside of his skin itch. He had started this by getting involved; he would finish it. It had nothing to do with the new attraction he felt for Faith, or the idea that one of the other guys would be down the hall from her while she wore those cute pajamas.

"You're not going to call anyone, are you?" Sloane's voice drove him back to their living room. "You're not going to ask for someone else to take over this assignment. You competitive bastard. You would rather risk your niece's safety than admit defeat."

"That's not what this is. You and Cleo are safe as long as I'm here. That's why I brought Faith over. With everyone under the same roof, and one of my teammates stationed outside the house, we'll be fine while I help Faith figure out who's after her and what they want."

Sloane pulled her phone from her back pocket

and tapped at the screen. "Jen, can Cleo and I spend the night?" She waited while Jen spoke. "No, but I'll explain later. Thanks." She ended the call.

"Sloane, please don't go. I'll feel better knowing where you are, and you're being looked after."

"Listen up, brother of mine, I don't need you to keep an eye on me or my daughter. I will take her to Jen's where she and I will be plenty safe with Jen's huge German shepherd. When this little charade of bodyguard and damsel in distress is over, call me. I will return to my home."

Sloane marched up the steps. In less time than it took for water to drain out of a tub, she was back with a sleeping Cleo in her arms and two bags over her shoulders.

"At least let me help you get in the car."

She pressed her lips together, but she didn't say no. He would take that as a victory. She didn't say one word to him while he buckled Cleo into her car seat, but the rigidness of Sloane's body said it all. He kissed the top of Cleo's head and ducked out of the car. The cold air bit through his thin shirt. He pounded his feet to get the circulation moving.

Sloane tossed the bags into the trunk and slid into the driver's seat. "Step away so I don't run over your foot."

He didn't budge. "I'm sorry. I didn't mean for you to leave the house." He didn't want to have to choose sides. He could take care of everyone, but he knew

Sloane would do what she wanted no matter how much he fought her.

"I don't know how you could expect me to stay with her in there."

"It's my job."

"No, it's your ego. Lincoln, Jax, or Quint could've watched her. Why does it have to be you?"

"We're a newer team. I offered to handle this pro bono. I can't go back on my word." There were a million excuses he could give her. But the real reason was simply that he wanted to help Faith. She had awakened something in him he thought was dormant. He needed to take a risk and see if it could be anything more than wishful thinking.

She shook her head and backed the car down the driveway. He stood there until she turned the corner and was out of sight.

He glanced at the Faith's house. He had better be right about this, or Sloane would never forgive him. And if Faith moved away, leaving him behind with only his Christmas decorations, what would he have to show for it?

## CHAPTER 13

Faith had to get out of that room. She didn't care what Zane had said about staying put. She needed air. Grabbing her coat, she made her way through his bedroom without stopping to inspect every surface for clues to the life he led.

The heady scent of spice and soap drifting around the wake of air she created as she dodged the corner of the king-size bed made her head spin. Of course, his smell would be sexy, and full, like a strong cup of tea.

Her knee caught the corner of the bed. She leapt forward like a dancer out of practice and collided with the solid chest of one Zane Cutler. He gripped her arms and steadied her before she could tumble to the ground.

"Are you okay?" He eased her away but kept his hands on her arms.

Her skin tingled in the places he touched. What else could those hands accomplish? She shook her head, forcing herself to focus on the mission to get air and not get into his bed.

"You're not okay? Is it your leg?" He reached for her leg.

She moved back. "Yes. No. I mean, I am okay. Thank you." As okay as she could be with all that was happening.

"Where were you going? I told you to stay here." The concern that had passed over his dark eyes was replaced with the emotionless glare.

"I needed some air. It's too small in that room."

"You could've opened the window."

"Not the same thing." She wanted to make something right tonight if it was the last thing she did. "I'm sorry about all of this. I didn't mean for you to fight with Sloane. Call her back. I'll find another way to deal with my problem." She didn't want to be the person that came between family. She would never have a chance with Zane if Sloane didn't like her. A sister had to always approve of the girlfriend.

She needed to get her head on straight. Nothing could happen between her and Zane. She couldn't even tell him the whole truth. After what happened at the Christmas tree farm, he wouldn't be interested in her if he ever was.

"Sloane will get over it. She's heated right now. That's the way she operates. Get mad first, think second. It's a Cutler family curse." The smile made a small reappearance on his face.

Her shoulders took a rest from holding up her ears. "Are you sure?"

"Yeah. Come downstairs. I'll make us something to eat, and you can fill me in on your past."

"I'm not hungry."

"Well, I am." He took her hand.

That simple gesture shouldn't give her so much comfort, but his strong grip around hers made her want to bury herself in the protection of his arms. It had been so long since anyone else carried the burden of her emotions for her. Her parents were the last people she could rely on, and they weren't very good at emotional support.

"Sit." He pointed to the kitchen table. The word wasn't filled with a command, but with an understanding that he would take the lead.

"I think I might prefer to stand. Too much nervous energy. Is there something I can help you with?"

"Do you drink wine?"

"Sure."

"There's a bottle of white in the fridge. Sloane only drinks white. Glasses in the cabinet above your head. Pour yourself a big glass, and tell me who these people are that are after you."

"Then what?"

He cocked an eyebrow. "Then you let me handle

whatever happens next. I'm the expert."

She opened the refrigerator door and let the cool air soothe her heated skin. His statement and the mischievous look in his eye dared her to think about things better left for the privacy of her room.

"Do you want some?" Her voice cracked against her dry throat. She held up the wine bottle, not to have to say more.

"I'm more of a beer guy. Also, in the fridge, if you don't mind opening one. No glass. Now, Faith, no more stalling. Tell me."

She didn't know where to begin. The moment she found out her parents were jewelry thieves? Or the night of the murder when she came home and found them dead? She rummaged through the drawers with shaking hands and searched out a bottle opener.

Zane left his pots on the stove and produced what she needed from a drawer by the sink she had ignored. Their fingers brushed as he handed over the opener. The electric current from the touch to her brain short-circuited what she was about to say. She sipped wine instead.

"Let me make this easier for you. I'm going to get straight to the point. Were your parents into selling and dealing drugs?"

She dropped into the chair by the table. "It's probably easier I just tell you instead of you asking questions. You aren't going to like what you hear. I never did."

"You have my attention." He put a lid on the pot and gripped his beer, but didn't drink.

She turned the wine glass in circles. "My parents weren't your ordinary kind of parents. They were more like parents that television studios made shows about, except this was real life weirdly enough."

He sat opposite her and stilled the glass. "Before you spill it." The smile returned to his handsome face.

"My parents stole jewelry for a living." There. She had said it out loud to the first person ever. No one knew that. Not her best friend from high school, though Faith suspected she knew something was different about their family. Her ex-boyfriend didn't know that. Her agent didn't know. No one did.

"This must've been big-time stuff. Millions of dollars. Right?" He hadn't flinched as if he heard that kind of thing every day.

"They had several scams working. I didn't know everything. And I suspect jewelry wasn't the only thing they stole or dealt in. I just never tried to prove it. When I asked questions about their work, they always put me off. They didn't want me to know, but I did." And she hated them for it. She had wanted to be a regular family more than anything in the world. Kind of like the family Zane had.

"They kept you from what they did?"

"They wanted to protect me. That's what they said anyway. At least that was during one of our last conversations. I can't know who killed them or why.

I was just worried they would come looking for me some day."

"And they have."

"Appears that way. I would give them what they wanted if I really knew, but I don't. I don't even have stuff from my childhood. The only things I kept were some dumb Christmas decorations my mom and I bought when I was little."

"Christmas decorations are never dumb. Especially when you're a kid. Cleo loves pulling out all the boxes and lining our ornaments up on the floor. She wants to see them all before she decides which ones go on the tree first."

"That's sweet. Cleo is adorable." Being around that little girl made her long for a family of her own more than ever.

"When I was about five or six, my mother bought me my own artificial tree. She let me pick out all my own decorations. But by the time I was ten, I had had enough of my small tree with things hanging from it that didn't really matter. My mother loved her fancy tree with her expensive ornaments. All of which she probably stole." Her mother had wanted a tree that could impress people when they came over. The ruse to buy her a tree of her own was so Faith wouldn't mess up the well-placed display.

She still remembered the joy filling her up like helium when her mother took her to the store to buy the ornaments. They came home, and her father joined them to decorate. They sang Christmas carols and drank hot cocoa. That was a tradition they continued for years. Until she stopped it because she was tired of the lies. Tired of her parents.

"Hey, it's okay." Zane slipped his hand over hers and gave a squeeze.

She blinked away tears she didn't even realize had formed. The walk down memory lane and the time with Zane and his family broke apart the wall she'd so carefully built to protect her heart. "I don't think it ever was. How do I make these people stop?"

"I don't know yet. But I'll figure it out. I have members of my team keeping an eye on us all night. If someone returns to leave another card, or something else, they'll be stopped. I promise you that."

He returned to the stove and stirred what was quickly becoming a dinner that smelled of comfort and home. She missed his touch and sat on her hands to keep from getting up and touching him more.

"Whoever is after me isn't going to go away." That was a fact as much as it was a fact it snowed in December in Montana.

"No, they aren't. Did they leave a note the night of the murder?"

"Nothing. Our house had been ransacked. They were looking for something. Either my parents didn't have it, or they lied about not having it. I thought it must be a piece of jewelry or loose stones. Those, of course, are worth the most. I looked through everything, but I did it so fast I might have missed something."

"Do you still own the house?"

"I walked away completely. I guess the bank sold it. There may have been a mortgage." She hadn't bothered to find out. It wasn't hard to disappear. Not too many people in her parents' world even knew she existed. They had done that on purpose too.

"If the bank sold it, that rules out going back and looking unless your parents buried something in the walls." He scooped the spicy smelling food into bowls. Some splashed over the sides of the ladle and landed on his hand. He cursed under his breath and ran water over the spot already turning red.

"Are you okay?" She pushed out of the chair, but he waved her away.

"Fine. I've got this."

Typical male, but she didn't want to hurt his pride. She gave him the space he wanted.

"I doubt the present owners of my old house would appreciate us showing up with sledge hammers to break open walls. Unless we say we're filming a renovation show." She snapped her fingers at the possibility.

"Not the best idea." He arched a brow.

A flame of something better left unnamed took root in her veins as she watched him move around the kitchen with ease. He seemed to be comfortable no matter what he was doing. She wished she could say the same for herself.

"You're not exactly fun."

"I need to stay within the letter of the law, thank you very much." He refilled her wine glass. "If the people after you think you have what they want, then they may have already looked in the walls of your old house. That's why they're after you. You're their last hope."

"That would make sense. If they never found what they're looking for, it would stand to reason I have it."

"I'm going to ask you again, and I need you to be honest with me. Do you have what they want?"

"I'm not a liar. I might be a lot of things, but not that. I want to get on with my life. I want to stop running. I'm tired of being afraid all the time. I don't have what they want." A new kind of fire burned in her veins. She pushed her glass away.

He held up his hands. "Okay. Okay. I have to ask. It's my job." He turned back to the dinner bowls and garnished the meal with something green.

She drank in his broad shoulders that narrowed to a thin waist. His jeans hugged his tight butt and long legs. The anger at his probing question simmered down as she drank in the sight of him.

"How did you become a bodyguard?" The stress of the day and the fear ravaging her body tired her out and weighed on her already-exhausted shoulders.

The warmth in the kitchen and the man in the room only made her want to curl up on the sofa with Zane and fall asleep with her head on his shoulder.

He brought over two bowls filled with stew and bread he had warmed up in the microwave. He took his seat again and tapped his bottle to her wine glass. "Eat up."

She took a big inhale of the comfort food and let her mouth water. The spoon hovered halfway between her mouth and the bowl. "You didn't answer my question."

He leaned back in the seat. "How did I become a bodyguard? Long story. The short one is I was in the army. I watched a lot of men and women I admired and liked get killed or maimed. I got hurt while on duty enough to be discharged. While working at a warehouse, I met Hank Patterson. He's the man that runs the Brotherhood. He hired me. The rest is history."

What she suspected he meant was the rest was none of her business. That was fine. Everyone had their secrets. She did.

They finished the meal in easy silence. To think only a short time ago, she wanted to get out of the house and be anywhere else, but after spending time with Zane and enjoying a meal together as if they'd done it a hundred times before, the only place she wanted to be was right where she was.

Her phone rang.

Zane flinched when the ear-piercing ring interrupted their dinner. He had been so wrapped up in the ease of the conversation with Faith he'd forgotten he was actually working. Bad move on his part. He wouldn't make that mistake again.

Faith fumbled with her phone. She stared at the screen while the device continued to make noise. Her mouth formed a small "oh." Her full bottom lip stuck out just enough it made him want to run his tongue over it and see if she tasted salty and spicy like the stew. He needed to know.

"Excuse me a second." Faith pushed away from the table and went outside to take the call.

He glanced at the back door. Her silhouette paced back and forth. He shot Lincoln a text to make sure the perimeter of the house had been checked.

*All good.* Lincoln wrote back.

At least Faith would be safe while she handled whatever was happening on that call. He should bring her a jacket, but clearly, she didn't want him anywhere near that call. It could be from an ex or maybe a distant family member. If it were from the people leaving the cards, he hoped she'd tell him. Her personal life could stay hidden, but the threats had to be out in the open or he couldn't help her.

He cleaned up the dishes and pots while she stayed outside. They did need to get to the bottom of what was happening, but he wanted to return to the ease of their dinner. He liked spending time with her. He also liked the challenge of opening her eyes up to Christmas.

Earlier today before everything went bad, her shoulders had dropped, and she smiled and laughed with Cleo as they ran from tree to tree deciding which one to pick.

He had always thought sharing Cleo with Sloane as the best uncle on the planet was enough for him. But today when he watched Cleo and Faith, he wondered how much different it would be to have a child of his own.

He shot Sloane a text to see if she and Cleo were okay. She wrote back they were fine, and he could go fuck himself. He smiled. She wouldn't stay mad at him.

Faith stood in the doorway, wiping her hands on her legs. Her cheeks were red from the cold. Her eyes had grown wide as if she'd seen a ghost. "Sorry about that."

"Is everything okay?" He leaned against the counter to give her space and a chance to tell him what was happening so they could sit back down and reconnect.

"It was my agent. I had called her earlier. Is there anymore wine?" She stepped farther into the kitchen. Her gaze searched the table that now sat void of their dinner. Something like disappointment swept over her eyes.

"I can open a new bottle. Did your agent have bad news?" He didn't know anything about the book writing business, but from the way she picked at the cuffs of her shirt, he would guess that call didn't go well for her.

"Don't bother. I'll make tea instead. If that's okay." She moved around the table toward the stove.

"I'll take care of it. Sit." Even if this was technically a job, he wanted to make the wide-eyed stare go away. During dinner she had relaxed. Her smile had been present the whole time. She had practically reclined in the chair as if they were sitting at the beach and not in his kitchen, wondering when the next Christmas card would arrive.

"I'd rather stand." Her body was ram rod straight. She returned to the other side of the table and took a few steps before turning on her heel and walking back.

"What did your agent say?" He put water in the tea kettle Sloane left on the stove. He didn't understand his sister's fascination with tea. It was just colored water to him with no taste. He preferred his coffee.

She turned her gaze on him. "I'm sorry. I missed what you said."

"Your agent. The phone call."

"Oh that. I can't talk about it. It's a contract thing.

Plus, it's boring. You wouldn't be interested in book publishing."

"Would my sister have read any of your books? She loves to read. Reads all the time." He poured the water from the whistling kettle into a mug for her and dunked the bag like he'd seen Sloane do.

"I'm not that popular." She took the mug from him but avoided his gaze.

Their fingers grazed as he handed off the cup. Her fingers were cold from the outside, but the electricity from their touch ignited a hot flame in his chest. He tried to meet her stare, but she kept her eyes down. The current between them, or maybe just coming from his direction, cooled down.

"I'll have her look you up online."

"She won't want to read my stuff. I'm not that good." She waved his suggestion away like cigarette smoke and put the table between them.

"I think you're being overly modest. Isn't writing how you make your living?"

"It is." She sipped at the tea.

"Then you must be decent. Let's go in the family room. I can start a fire."

"No, thank you. I think I'll head up to bed. Thank you for dinner. I'll be out of your hair in the morning."

"What does that mean?" Her sudden one-eighty made his head spin.

"You can't keep protecting me. I've caused too

much trouble. I'll figure things out." She headed toward the hallway.

"Hang on a second." He grabbed her arm to stop her.

"Please, Zane. I've caused enough pain. I don't want to bring you or your family any more."

"I don't understand. We were just getting along really well. Was it something your agent said? Were you actually talking to your agent? If it was the people leaving the cards on the phone, you need to tell me."

She shrugged her shoulders on a long breath. "It was my agent. I promise. You and I getting along doesn't matter. My life is too complicated to have you dragged in any further. I'll go back to my house in the daylight if that's okay. After that, you're fired."

## CHAPTER 14

FAITH TRIED to convince herself to go back to her own house. There was nothing to be afraid of. Zane's team was outside. They'd watch all night. So, why was she having such trouble grabbing that bag of hers and going?

She put the tea mug down on the small table beside the bed. Zane made her feel safe. Something she hadn't known in a long time. For one more night, she wanted to sleep, or at least try to sleep, with ease. As long as he was in the house with her, nothing would happen. Starting tomorrow, she'd have to find other ways to feel safe.

All this waiting around made her crazy. The people after her were torturing her with their messages. Maybe that was the plan. If she lost her mind from fear and worry, then she would hand over what they wanted. Joke was on them. She didn't have it.

These crazy people would show themselves eventually. When they did, she hoped she was ready. Which made Molly's call earlier an even bigger problem. Her publisher sent out a newsletter saying Mac Addison would be at the Missoula Barnes and Noble. They were already selling tickets.

She would have to finish the entire novel in time and show her face on every media platform without knowing if the bad guys were caught. It would only take seconds for anyone with a handful of knowledge about the web to figure out Mac Addison was Faith Rudolph. Who was really Faith Karla. Her parents were Jean and Tom Karla. They owned a jewelry store on Seventh. Everyone in town loved them and trusted them. What everyone didn't know about was the multi-million-dollar scams going on in the back of Karla's Jewelry.

She could never tell Zane her real name. Then he'd be able to find out she was involved in her parents' murder. At least now, he would think of her as a nut-job who cared about his family.

She saw the way he looked at her during dinner. The heat in the air wasn't coming from the stew. It may have been a while since she'd been with a man, but she still recognized the signs. The desire in his dark eyes that turned them into a pool of liquid would have to be enough for her fantasies. She could never have Zane. Ever.

A knock on the door made her jump. "Faith, it's me. Can you open up?"

She opened the door to Zane standing in the shadows of his room. The light from the hallway casted a glow behind him. Her lamp on the side table gave her enough light to see the confusion in his eyes.

"Is everything okay?" She wrapped her arms around her middle as some kind of pathetic barrier between them.

"You need to tell me. Why did you run away?" He leaned his head against the doorjamb. The lines around his mouth suggested he was as tired as she was.

"I told you."

"I know what you said, but that isn't the whole story. You're trying to protect me from something, but you don't have to do that. I can take care of myself just fine. I'm here to keep you safe." He rubbed the ends of her hair between his fingers.

She should back away and shut the door. Being with him would only cause him and his family harm. She couldn't live with herself if she was the reason another family was hurt. She wasn't worth it for someone to love. She caused destruction in her wake. Her relationships had failed. She let her parents down.

Her hands moved before she could stop them and

traced the five o'clock shadow dotting his strong jaw. The stubble against her sensitive fingertips made her belly tingle. She wanted to know what his beard would feel like against her cheeks, her breasts, and other spots she needed to not think about or her knees might go weak. How selfish would it be to ask for one night?

He closed his eyes and on a long breath he leaned into her touch. "This is crazy," he said.

She yanked her hand back. His eyes flew open.

"I'm sorry. I shouldn't have..." She pushed the door closed.

His palm smacked the wood stopping it midway. "No. What's crazy is how I'm feeling. I have never become involved with a client before. Never even thought about it. But you, from the moment I saw you something was different...." His words trailed off in a whisper.

She didn't need him to say any more. The connection had been there for her too. Even his silly Christmas decorations couldn't dissuade her. The more she was near him, the more she wanted to be. "When we first met, I wasn't a client."

Her hands cupped his face and brought him closer to taste his lips. They were cool with the remnants of beer on them. She curled her fingers into his hair to take the kiss deeper. He opened his mouth, knowing what she wanted.

His arms circled her waist and pressed her against

him. His desire on her belly was unmistakable. A shiver ran over her skin. Reason tried to exert itself in her brain. Sleeping with a man she had just met was not smart. Getting involved with her bodyguard and keeping secrets from him would only lead to heartbreak. But the wild abandon of her heart drove reason away.

"Faith, are you sure?" He eased away from the kiss and looked down at her.

She was grateful for the shadows to hide behind. "I've never done anything like this before. Slept with someone I hardly know." But she wanted to now. More than she wanted anything else.

"I didn't think you had." He brushed a stray hair away from her face.

"How can you tell something like that?" She ran her finger along the collar of his shirt. She wanted to touch the skin beneath it.

"The uncertainty in your eyes. It's been there since dinner. If you hadn't kissed me, I would have chalked your look up to worry about the cards or bad stew."

A small laugh bubbled over her lips, and he laughed too. His laugh went deep into his chest and eased the concerns from her mind.

He tilted her chin up, forcing her to look at him. "You don't have to be afraid with me. I promise we will only do what you say. If that's standing here making out all night and nothing else, then that's all it is." He kissed the side of her jaw by her ear.

Her knees went weak for sure. She had plenty of other ideas besides standing in the doorway kissing. "Take me to bed."

ZANE COULDN'T BELIEVE his ears, but he wasn't going to pass up the opportunity. He scooped Faith up in his arms and carried her to his bed which was much bigger than the small daybed in the room she was using.

"You didn't have to carry me." She laughed as he laid her down and climbed on the bed beside her.

"I thought women liked that kind of thing."

"Maybe if they broke a leg."

"Duly noted. No more carrying you anywhere." He wanted to taste her again. He had been right about her lips being spicy and salty.

She giggled, and his heart soared. He wanted to make her laugh all day long, and when this thing with the cards was over, he would go on making her laugh. If she wanted him to, that was. Maybe after all of this she would move away again. He would need to be ready for that. It would be in his best interest to lock some of his heart away so she couldn't completely obliterate it.

He kissed her again. Her mouth opened willingly

for him while her hands trailed down his back. His skin seared from her touch. He wanted her hands all over his body, but he didn't want to rush her. He would let her take the lead. He meant what he said. She made the rules.

His lips sought out her neck. He caught a hint of her lavender perfume tucked under her hair.

"That's nice," she said.

"Glad you like it." He continued his descent to her collarbone.

Her hands went under his shirt. He sucked in a breath as she explored his chest, drawing lines with her fingertips. Her touch was cool, but it still left fire in its wake.

He would wait for the invitation to touch her bare skin, but his hand found her breast and caressed it through the material of her sweater. He felt the anticipation of wanting more like he did in high school with his first girlfriend who would not let him get to second base until they were dating three months.

She pushed away and sat up breaking the connection.

"What's the matter?" Had he done something wrong?

She brushed the hair away from his face and left her palm on his cheek. "We have too many clothes on."

She grabbed the bottom of her sweater and lifted

it over her head revealing a lacy navy-blue bra. His breath caught on his desire.

"You're beautiful."

"Thank you. So are you." She tugged at the bottom of his shirt.

He didn't wait but pulled the thing over his head. Her smile reached her eyes and lit up her face. Her finger drew a straight line down the center of his chest and rested at the top of his jeans.

"I like the way you touch me." He wanted her hands all over him and he wanted to feel her respond to his touch as well. He wasn't sure if he would be able to slow down enough.

"Can I touch you more?" She worked her lip under her teeth.

He was a goner for sure. "Anywhere you want."

FAITH TRIED to slow her heart, but the damn thing banged around like cans being dragged from the back of a speeding car. She hadn't been with a man in a long time. What if she forgot what to do? Or worse, what if Zane didn't like her moves?

Since her parents' deaths, she calculated every risk, planned all her moves. In the end it didn't get her much. Tonight, she wanted to let go completely and enjoy what was happening right in front of her with a very sexy man.

She leaned closer to kiss him again. He wrapped an arm around her shoulders and pulled her against his strong chest. Her hands roamed over his back. She relished the feel of his flexing muscles against her touch. She sunk her hands right inside the waist band of his jeans. He moaned.

Pride gave her the courage to push him back on the bed and explore the angles and lines of his chest with her tongue. He tasted smooth and salty. His fingers tangled in her hair as her mouth went lower.

She should stop this whole thing and tell him the truth about the night her parents died. He would feel differently about her if he knew, but he unhooked her bra and obliterated reason when he cupped her breast. She stopped her delicious tasting party to slip the fabric from her arms.

He would never have to know. They would stop the bad guys; she would move away to somewhere else, and he would never be the wiser. She would have this night to fold away like a love letter in a secret box. She could pull it out whenever she needed to revisit it.

"Faith, you're driving me crazy with that tongue." His voice was low but gritty with desire.

She circled his navel with the tip of her tongue. One hand traveled back up his chest and rubbed his nipple. He let out a long sigh. So far so good. Her other hand explored the tight muscles of his thighs through the thick fabric of his jeans. More clothes would need to go soon.

He found her breast again while she returned to memorizing the taste of his hip bone. He rubbed her nipple between his fingers. Her breath picked up speed. A moan escaped her lips. She wanted his hands everywhere.

Just the way he seemed to be able to read all her signs earlier, he read her mind now. He pulled her up and kissed her on the lips. "I need to touch you now. Is that okay?"

"Yes." Her voice was a croak.

He slid her pants over her hips. Nothing was left except her panties. He shimmied out of his jeans and tossed them aside. His arousal was evident. The knowledge that she was the reason for it put a smile on her face.

Climbing back on the bed, he positioned himself between her legs. His gaze held hers. "Still okay?"

"You're very considerate." More so than any other man she'd been with. She could fall hard for Zane, if only their lives had intersected somewhere else.

"I don't want you to have any regrets. You've been through enough. You don't need to feel any pressure from me. I can put my clothes back on right now."

"Don't you dare." She would never regret this night. No matter how things turned out.

"I was kind of hoping you'd say that." He offered her a lopsided grin.

Her heart knocked harder on her ribs. She pulled him to her and kissed him again with a renewed energy. She wanted him and hoped he understood how much.

His hands were all over her. He slid one down her belly and removed the last of her clothing. She tucked her hands inside his boxers and tugged them low enough he could get them out of the way.

His hand hesitated near her thigh. She pushed it closer to the spot that ached to be touched by him. Sliding his finger inside her, he brought that ache to a new level. Her hips moved to get more. A moan escaped her lips.

He pulled his mouth away from hers to growl in her ear. "I guess that means you like what I'm doing?"

"Very much."

He changed the rhythm of his touch inside her. Her hips responded and matched him beat for beat. She had written love scenes in her books a thousand times. Each time wondering if passion that set every nerve ending raw, and an insatiable, growing desire was a real thing. Now she knew. The ache wouldn't go away with just what they were doing. She needed more of him.

"Zane?"

"Hmm?" His mouth had found her breast. He sucked and nipped, making her head spin.

"This might be a bad time to ask…." She didn't

want to kill the mood, but they didn't really know each other.

He pushed up on his forearms and met her gaze. The lopsided grin was back. "This sounds like a personal question is coming."

"I don't want to know how many women you've been with if that's what you mean."

"I would tell you."

"Maybe some other time." She didn't want to know how many people she was competing with. "I didn't come prepared, if you know what I mean."

"Got it covered. Bad joke." He laughed and rolled to the side of the bed. He rummaged around in the side table and held up his prize.

She laughed too. He made everything easy. She had never known a life filled with ease and joy. He lived each moment to its fullest. She shrunk from life all the time.

He returned to her and kissed her again. The heat and the ache moved to the next level.

"Are you ready?" he said.

She took him in her hand and stroked. He lined up their bodies. With a thrust, he was inside her, filling her up. They moved together. Slow at first learning their way. But the pace increased until they were panting, and sweat beaded her body.

She wasn't sure she would make it to the end. The ache coiled into a tight rope but would not break and set her free. This time would be like every other because she wasn't being truthful.

"Don't give up." He whispered in her ear.

Her breath caught. He slipped his hand between them and touched her most sensitive spot. She let out a gasp, but he continued to caress her.

The coil inside her snapped. She soared end over end, gripping his back as he thrust inside her until he too had come to the end.

## CHAPTER 15

FAITH COULDN'T SLEEP. After their lovemaking, Zane had nodded off, but her mind still raced around too many bad thoughts. She slipped from the covers and dragged his shirt over her head. His woodsy smell clung to the fabric. She brought the collar to her nose and took a long inhale.

The room was chilly. The warmth of his arms around her was much nicer, but she didn't want to disturb him with all her tossing and turning. She went to the window and peered out. Snow fell in large, puffy flakes. His room looked out onto the front of the yard. His Christmas lights were off, but the glow of the snow offered enough light to see. A pickup truck sat across the street. That was probably part of his team keeping them safe all night. He should've invited them in. They must be freezing.

But she might not have been so willing to go to bed with him if anyone else was in the house. She needed the isolation to be brave enough. Her body tingled remembering the way he touched her. The memory would have to do. It wasn't likely they would sleep together a second time.

Zane rolled over. He muttered something, but she couldn't make out what it was. His legs kicked under the sheets. With her eyes adjusted to the dark, she moved closer to him. His face was twisted in pain or confusion. His lips continued to move, but only every other word came out.

"Don't go," he said, but his eyes remained tightly closed.

She took another step closer to the bed, unsure if she should wake him. His hair stuck in wet strands to his forehead. The room was too cold for him to be sweating.

"Zane?"

He continued to mutter.

"Zane?" She tried louder this time.

"Not that way," he said.

His legs continued to kick under the sheets. Whatever was bothering him, he might not want her to know about. They hadn't spent enough time together to share some of their deeper stuff. Nightmares would definitely count for that.

She placed a hand on his shoulder. He jerked up and yelled. She jumped.

"Zane, are you okay?"

"What happened?" His voice was coated with sleep. He wiped a hand over his face.

"I think you were having a bad dream. I'm sorry if I woke you; I didn't want you to go on like that." She backed up to the window to give him some space and the cover of darkness.

"You didn't wake me."

"But you sat up and yelled when I put a hand on your shoulder." It was better she hadn't waited any longer to rouse him.

He flopped back on the bed. "That wasn't your fault. Was I talking in my sleep?"

"A little."

"Come here." He waved her over.

She didn't move.

"Faith, please come back to bed." He propped up on an elbow. Even in the dark, she could tell he was smiling.

She eased over to his side of the bed and tucked a leg under her. He rubbed her thigh with his fingers. The sensation warmed her like a good fire.

"I was having a nightmare. It's no big deal."

"Do you want to talk about it?"

He gripped her knee. "No." His curt voice made her flinch.

She got up.

"Where are you going?" he said.

"Just here." Back by the window. A safer distance.

STACEY WILK

She shouldn't be upset that he didn't want to talk about his dream. They weren't anything except a convenience at the moment. They both were attracted. Tension had been high. Having sex made sense to dispel some of that tension. Still, she wanted him to be able to trust her with how he was feeling. The intimacy they shared meant something to her.

"Please come back to bed. I'm sorry about being abrupt." He patted the bed.

She stayed put.

"Please, Faith. I didn't mean to sound like a jerk."

She eased her way back to her side of the bed and sat down. He gathered her in his arms and kissed her head. She leaned into him, unable to stop herself. The warmth of their bodies and his woodsy scent eased the tension from her shoulders. She could get used to this.

"My shirt looks good on you." He whispered into her hair.

"Thanks. I hoped you wouldn't mind." She wasn't sure he even noticed and was glad he had.

"You can wear my shirt and sleep in my bed anytime."

She sucked in her breath. That sounded like an invitation, but did she dare risk the question? He could be trying to distract her from how he was feeling about having a nightmare in front of her.

"That's very gentlemanly of you." Even if he was

inviting her for another night, he probably said that to every woman he made love to.

"I don't invite just anyone to sleep over."

She pushed back to see his face. How many women had been in this bed? And how long ago? She should have asked before she went so willingly. He could think of her as nothing more than a conquest or a tension reliever. "Why is that?"

"It's been a while since I slept all night with any woman. I haven't wanted to wake up beside anyone."

Her heart lodged in her windpipe. "I understand." She untangled herself from his grasp.

"Hey, wait a second." He reeled her back in and held her closer. "I didn't mean you. You are the first woman in a long time I wanted to spend the whole night with. You make me feel things I thought I would never feel again."

Her heart stayed lodged in her throat. "Zane, I feel the same about you, but how can that be right?"

"I don't know. But it is, and that's all I care about for the moment. We can figure out the rest when we catch the Christmas card stalkers."

She should tell him the rest of her story now before anything between them went further. If he found out she was withholding information, he would not be happy. And her one chance at experiencing a real relationship might be over.

"Zane...I have something to tell you."

His phone lit up and vibrated against the side

table. "Hold that thought." He tapped her nose with his finger.

"Cutler." Zane swung his legs over the side of the bed.

She rolled onto her back and tugged the sheets to her neck. The softness of his shirt brushed against her skin. She really could make a habit of lying in bed with this man and sharing her thoughts. The control she had tried to place around her life was tilting like a stack of precarious boxes.

"How did that happen?" He pushed up and shoved his legs into his boxers. "Are you sure? Yeah, yeah. Okay. I'll be right down." He tossed the phone on the bed.

"What's the matter?" Her life tilted more.

"Get dressed. We need to go downstairs. I'm sorry." He grabbed a shirt from his dresser and tugged it over his head.

She stumbled from the bed, her legs getting caught in the blankets. "Zane, tell me what's going on." She searched for her clothes and scrambled into her panties and jeans.

"Come on." He didn't wait for her but hurried out of the room. His footsteps echoed off the hardwood stairs.

She followed in his wake. Her was stomach a massive knot of fear and uncertainty. She ran a hand through her tangled hair as if that would help control the chaos around her.

"What is it?" She tugged his shirt when she finally caught up to him in the kitchen.

A knock came at the back door. Her breath caught.

He opened it to a man she had never seen before. He was tall and well built. His dark hair hung to his shoulders. His eyes held a depth of wisdom and fatigue.

"Faith, this is my team leader Lincoln Smith."

"I'm sorry to barge in at such a late hour." Lincoln pulled his hand out from behind his back and handed Zane a red envelope.

She dropped into a chair. "Where was that?"

"I'm afraid it was left on Zane's porch this time. I'm sorry we didn't catch who left it. We had eyes on the house the whole time. Whoever did it was fast and silent. I saw the envelope when I got out of the truck to sweep the perimeter one more time."

"What about Jax?" Zane said.

"Jax was doing intel in the back seat. Not his fault. I gave Quint the night off. This is on me. I'll write up a report for Hank. I'm sorry, Ms. Rudolph. I won't drop the ball again."

"There is no need to apologize. Can I see the envelope please?" She went to Zane with her hand held out.

Zane handed it over. She debated on opening it or tossing it in the trash. Did it really matter what it said?

"There could be a clue to what they want inside there." Zane broke into her thoughts.

"There hasn't been so far," she said.

"Open it," Zane said.

She tucked her finger into the small opening where the flap met the back of the envelope and ripped. The sound echoed in the quiet and dark kitchen. The wind carried on outside the house as if it too thought the card was important.

The same cartoonish tree stared back at her. Her hands shook as she flipped the card open. *Your bodyguard can't keep you safe.*

She dropped the card, and it floated to the floor. "Why are they torturing me like this? Why not just attack me or break in?"

She wasn't sure how much more she could take. This whole thing needed to end.

"They want you off-balance," Lincoln said.

"You're more likely to cave to them if you start believing they're ready to pounce. I won't let you do that because no one accuses me of sucking at my job and gets away with it."

"So what do we do now?" she said.

Zane pulled three mugs from the cabinet and held them up. "I doubt anyone is getting any more sleep."

Lincoln took a mug. "We can't do anything until we know who we're dealing with. I searched for other investigations involving cards as communication, and nothing comes up."

"Did your parents have business partners?" Zane poured milk into his coffee.

"As far as I know, my parents didn't have any business partners. But they did have many friends. Or at least people I thought were friends." She took a mug and filled it with coffee just to warm her hands.

THEY USED to have dinner parties all the time when she was little. She would sit at the top of the stairs after she had gone to bed and hide in the shadows of the dark hallway to watch all the people. Women wore long gowns and miles of brilliant jewels. The men were all in expensive suits. Waiters in white gloves passed tall glasses of champagne. She would stay on the landing until she fell asleep. Her father would find her and carry her to bed. In the morning, it felt more like a dream.

After the murders, all those people that came to their dinner parties were nowhere to be found. No one had checked to see if she needed anything. She had been a college student, still a teenager, left on her own.

"Faith, you're going to have to try and remember anyone who stood out. Was your mom or dad angry about something before they died?" Zane put a hand on her arm. The touch warmed her insides like the coffee. She wanted this whole thing to go away and drown in the warmth he gave her.

The only fight she knew about was the one she had with them. "They didn't discuss their day to day activities with me. Whenever I confronted them about what they did for a living, they told me not to worry about it. The jewelry store they owned was just a front."

"Did you ever have proof?" Lincoln said.

"Nothing concrete. I suspected. Our lifestyle was too nice for owning that store. I saw how my friends from school lived and their parents had simple jobs too."

"Whatever happened to all the things in your house?" Zane said.

A phone ringing broke into the dark kitchen. Lincoln pulled it out of his back pocket and read the screen. "If you'll excuse me, I have to take this." He went outside.

"Sold. I guess. I don't know. A check arrived to me by courier one day. It was a decent amount of money. There was a note from my father's lawyer that said the money was mine. I didn't bother to question it. I figured he knew what he was doing. I invested the money. It was the least my parents could do for me. I know that sounds harsh but having jewelry thieves for parents was a tough nut to swallow."

"I can only imagine."

"I don't think you can." She placed the mug on the counter harder than she meant to. Coffee sloshed over the side and onto her hand. Zane narrowed his eyes.

He grabbed a dish towel and wrapped it around her hand. "Hey, I'm not trying to patronize you. I see the hurt in your eyes when you talk about them. I don't know what you're feeling. Sloane and I grew up in a pretty typical family. My parents supported us. My mom wasn't thrilled when I joined the army, but I didn't know what I wanted to do with my life, and college didn't seem like the answer. My dad just patted me on the back and told me to be careful. But they always made Christmas special for us. Sloane does that now for Cleo. I wish you had a different experience than you did with your parents. Maybe you'd be able to trust me now."

"What makes you think I don't trust you?" She didn't entirely, but that was because she'd spent her lifetime watching her own back. She couldn't possibly change that about herself in a few days no matter what this man said or made her feel.

"It's my job to read people. Earlier in bed, you gave over yourself, but out here now and every other minute, you watch me with a guarded eye. I really want to help you, but you have to help me with more information."

"I don't have any more. If I did, I would share it. There is nothing I know that could lead to finding this person or people."

The sun brightened the dark sky outside the

window. The branches of the trees swayed against a gray background. The chill in her bones would match the one outside. She may never be warm again. She didn't know how to convince Zane she had shared everything she knew.

Zane took her hand in his. "Then we wait for them to strike again. Hopefully, we'll be ready."

## CHAPTER 16

ZANE STARED at the Christmas decorations in Davis's yard. A long stream of cars came down the road and slowed each time. Davis had outdone himself this year by using the movie *White Christmas* as his backdrop.

Someone honked, and he turned. Bud Lewis rolled down the window of his patrol car. "You're going to lose, Cutler. Davis has a pretty good selection this year. What happened to you? Getting too old?" Bud laughed and moved on before Zane could even respond.

Ever since Faith showed up in his life, winning the competition wasn't in the forefront of his mind. He could give Davis a real run for his money, but he hadn't been as focused as years before.

He made his way back down the street. The snow began to drift around him and dust the ground. His feet kicked up flakes with each step. He burrowed further into his coat. Whoever was stalking Faith could be watching him right now. How many cards would be delivered before they did something rash? She had to know something.

He had searched for more information on her parents. Nothing came up for a Jean and Tom Rudolph. He needed to know what she was hiding. If she couldn't come clean with him, there would never be a future for them. Future? When had he started considering that? He'd sworn off relationships after his wife left him. She didn't want to be married to a wounded soldier who woke up screaming from his sleep.

He enjoyed his time with Faith in bed last night. Hell, he more than enjoyed it, but honesty was the most important thing to him. She was holding back information. He could feel it in his bones. He needed to get to the bottom of it now.

Sloane pulled into their driveway cutting him off. Her car shook up and down as it went over the lip of the asphalt. He hadn't expected to see her back so soon. He jogged to meet her coming out of the door.

"Uncle Zane." Cleo kicked her legs and wiggled around trying to undo the belt of her car seat.

Sloane blew the hair off her face and cocked a brow. "You're all she's been talking about. Hang on, sweetie. I'll help you out."

Cleo flung herself out of Sloane's arms and over

to him. He caught her midair. "Hey, kiddo. Welcome back."

"I missed you." Cleo wrapped her arms around his neck like a vise and her legs around his waist. Her hair smelled like bubble gum and soap. He held her tight against his chest and let the waves of how much he missed her wash over him.

"Are you back for good?" he said to Sloane.

She dragged her bags out of the trunk. "Looks that way. Is your friend still inside?"

"She went home to work. Linc is inside her house for extra security. Jax and Quint are watching the street." He debated on telling her about the card left on the porch but thought better of it. They were all safer with his team here, and Hank was on stand-by, ready to send in more Protectors if necessary.

More cars slid down the street to slow and watch all the lights. What if this time someone in one of those cars were the people after Faith? All the extra traffic made their street a risk. He should tell Sloane to go back to her friend's house. They'd be safer, but his team was watching, and no one was better than they were at what they did even minus the mistake last night.

He plopped Cleo on her feet and took the suitcase from Sloane. "Let's go inside and talk. It's freezing out here."

He locked the door behind them. "You hungry? I

can make us something. Maybe French toast for dinner?" He held up a spatula.

Cleo jumped up and down clapping her hands. Sloane cocked an eyebrow at him never happy about breakfast for dinner.

"Sweetie, go play in your room while I talk to Uncle Zane." Sloane hung her coat on the hook by the door.

"Will you read me a story tonight?" Cleo looked up at him with wide brown eyes and her mouth opened in a small circle.

"You betcha."

Cleo ran out of the room. Her footsteps echoed on the wooden stairs. He turned back to Sloane. "Go ahead and yell at me. You hate what I do for a living."

"Zane, I admire you and your job. So many people are safe in their beds at night because of you, but you brought danger into our home. I'm afraid to send Cleo to school."

"It's only a few days until the break, why don't you keep her home?" He pulled the ingredients out of the fridge and cabinets.

"She's looking forward to the holiday concert and party. I won't take that away from her, but I'm so mad I want to strangle you." She smacked the counter.

"I can send Jax to school with her. He'll sit in the desk next to her." His lips twitched at the idea of his partner shoving his tall frame into a kindergarten's desk.

"When is this going to be over?" Sloane scooped her hair away from her face.

"I don't know. Soon, I hope."

"Can't you send her someplace else? It's not like she owns that house. She can rent anywhere. You have safe houses, don't you?"

They had plenty of them scattered around the state. Even Linc's cabin at the top of the mountain acted as a place when they needed one. Linc kept his wife Serra there when she was in danger and the only ones who could help her were Linc and Jax.

Even if he did move Faith, his house was still at risk now. He didn't want to frighten his sister with that much truth. "I can't move her, but I won't bring her here anymore if that helps. I can always go next door to check on her."

"Why do you have to check on her?" Sloane took the egg out of his hand and cracked it over the bowl.

"Because she hired me to do it." And because he wanted to be with her. He could keep her safe, and she eased some of the hurt inside him.

"Your shoulder—"

"Is fine." He put a hand up.

Sloane narrowed her eyes. "Do you like her?"

He turned back to the butter sizzling in the pan and dipped bread in the milk mixture. "She's nice."

"Oh, no. You really like her. Why this one? There

have been a ton of women who have wanted to date you. Half of my friends, even, and you go and fall for the troubled one next door. That's just like you. Please tell me you haven't slept with her too."

He dropped the dripping slice of bread into the pan and ignored the question.

"Zane?"

He turned to match her fiery gaze. "My love life is none of your business just like yours is none of mine. That was our agreement for living together. If I want advice, I'll ask. In the meantime, don't worry about me."

With one hand on her hip, and the other tapping at the counter, she dropped her gaze for a second, but it raced back to collide with his. "I don't think I'm hungry anymore. Cleo and I will figure out dinner." She marched out of the kitchen.

"Sloane, come on." His voice fell on the floor unanswered.

He finished the French toast and left it wrapped on the stove for later. He wasn't hungry either, and he didn't want to stay in his house. It might've been better if Sloane had stayed away. It might have been even better if they never lived together.

He grabbed his coat and went across the yard to talk to his neighbor.

## CHAPTER 17

FAITH SLAMMED the computer shut and shoved out of the chair, knocking it over. The words wouldn't come. She had nothing left to say.

The competition in the publishing world was tough and few stayed on top for long. Her ride was over. She couldn't write. Didn't want to write. She wanted to solve her problems and start over somewhere.

She went to the window and pushed the curtain aside. Frost on the window outlined Zane's house like an antique photograph. He had been the first interesting thing in her life in a long time, but she'd be saying goodbye to that too. She smeared the frost on the glass.

Her thick socks padded against the carpet as she made her way from her office to her room. She didn't want to make any obvious noises. Lincoln Smith stood guard in her living room. Well, maybe he was sitting. She didn't know.

What she did know was it was time to go. She'd brought enough harm to too many people since she moved onto this lovely street with its dedicated residents. She would ruin everyone's holiday if she stayed. If she left, then maybe even the card senders wouldn't find her. At least for a little while. She'd figure out how to handle them herself which had been the original plan before all of this mess had started. She should have stuck to her plan.

This time when she made a run for it, she would throw her clothes and a few essentials into her suitcase and sneak out when Lincoln wasn't paying attention. It might be in the middle of the night when he was sleeping, but she could hang out until then. She wanted the two boxes in the basement that were the only tie to her past, but she couldn't risk going for them this time. Lincoln would hear her, and her chance to escape would be over.

She wrote a quick note to Zane explaining why she had to leave and thanking him for a wonderful night. No man made her body come to life like that. The simple thank you scooped a hole in her heart, but it was all she had to give him. She could hope he would miss her, but she would settle for the occasional kind thought about her every Christmas.

A knock on the front door made her breath catch in her throat. She shoved the note inside the top drawer of her dresser and forced her breathing to continue in a regular manner.

"I've got it," Lincoln said from the bottom of the steps.

Muffled voices drifted up to her. Another man was in the house. The absence of fighting sounds made her fists unclench. That was the conversation of two people comfortable with each other. Zane was probably down there. She snuck back into her office, righted the chair she had knocked over, and opened up her computer again. At least she could feign an attempt at being productive if someone came looking for her. It also solved the problem of no one seeing her suitcase being open on the bed.

"Can we talk?" Zane tapped on the doorjamb with his knuckles. His smile spread wide on his face revealing his perfect teeth. His shrugged out of his jacket.

His broad shoulders wrapped in a green Henley and his thin waist reminded her of last night when nothing was between them except the sweat on their bodies.

Her own smile burst open before she could remind it to play things cool. She crossed the room and wrapped her arms around his neck. His presence was the one thing that made her feel as if she could stop running. Even with that suitcase ready in the other room, she wanted to be in Zane's arms where anything seemed possible. Anything like a chance at a real life. Wasn't she entitled to that?

"Have you ever wanted to completely let go? Hold nothing back and just see what happens?" Asking a question like that only led to a dangerous answer, but for once she didn't want to be afraid. Zane would not allow fear to get in his way.

"Do you mean like sky diving or something?" He wrapped his arms around her waist and pulled him against his strong chest.

"No, I mean just give up whatever holds you back. Let the fear disappear like the fog." She'd been running away from fear her whole life, hoping it wouldn't catch up to her. It did. Every time.

"Some fear keeps us safe. Like that tingling on your skin when you walk through a parking lot alone at night. That's what tells you to turn around and get the security guard. But that's not what you're talking about it, is it?"

"Does anything scare you?" She placed a hand on his chest. His heart kept time under her touch. Her own heart matched the rhythm.

"Some things." His voice was smooth and low and deep-coated with intensity. His gaze locked on hers.

A delicious shiver ran over her skin. The idea of leaving this man fought hard to remain in the front of her mind. "Like what?"

"Like the way you seem to make me forget logic when we're together. You are an unexpected surprise.

The last gift under the Christmas tree that got pushed to the back and almost left unopened."

It would be so easy to let go with him. She read trust in his eyes, or at least that's what she hoped was there. To have someone to share her worries with would untie the rope around her chest always choking the breath from her lungs. There would be a price to pay for giving away trust. There always was.

"Did I say too much?" He kissed her jaw near her ear.

"My feelings for you frighten me too. I shouldn't feel anything. I hardly know you." Except every nerve ending charged with electricity as his tongue made small circles on her skin.

"I hope last night made you feel something. I'm pretty sure you were enjoying it as much as I was." He continued a trail down her neck.

An unrestrained giggle bounced over her lips. She angled her head to meet his lips.

He cupped the back of her head and kept her close. His mouth was on hers possessing her. She opened up to him and chased his tongue with hers. He tasted like sweet butter and wanted more.

He moaned as his other hand slid down her spine and rested on her bottom. She needed to be closer and pressed her chest against his. The start of his erection was evident against her low belly. Her hands ran under his shirt. The warmth of his skin managed to set hers on fire.

The pounding of footsteps on the stairs broke them apart.

"Whoa, sorry." Lincoln stopped short. "I was just wondering when you were leaving for that ride. I guess there's been a change in plans." He turned on the step.

"Linc—" Zane began

"Nope. It's all good. No explaining." Lincoln trotted down the steps.

"What did he mean about a ride?"

"I wanted to take you for a ride so we could talk. I need to go after him. He didn't know how I felt about you. I have to reassure him I have good judgment where the case is concerned." He grabbed his jacket.

"I have to get back to work anyway."

"Can I come back later? Maybe after he goes to sleep?" The side of his lip curled in a knowing smile.

"I'll wait up for you."

She had everything to lose and nothing to gain by continuing this thing with Zane. Her heart wouldn't stand to be torn to bits when this man's affection was no more.

But she would unpack that suitcase anyway.

## CHAPTER 18

ZANE FOUGHT with the hand truck to move the giant Christmas ornaments in front of the bushes. The tires made ruts in the snow, but the uneven ground provided obstacles every two feet for him to get stuck in. He stopped and blew on his hands.

The gun-metal gray sky kept the temperature just above freezing. A storm was due in by tonight, threatening to dump three feet this time. He wanted Faith to sleep at his house in case the street lost power. He had a generator. She didn't. Whoever was watching her would know she was alone and defenseless.

When Cleo got home from school, he would grab Faith and with Sloane they would decorate the tree. He smiled thinking about the way Faith moved under him last night after he snuck into her house so Linc wouldn't know he was there. They tried to be quiet with Lincoln asleep on the couch, but when Zane came down the steps holding his boots long before the sun even thought about rising, Linc was already at the coffee maker with a smirk on his face.

The street was quiet this time of day when mothers ran home to meet the bus. The traffic to see the decorations was nothing more than a drip. But tonight, the cars would pick back up if the snow hadn't come. He had checked the town's Facebook page. Their street was in second place to Maria Emerson's. That was why he went out and bought the ornaments. He needed to add to his yard. This year his display was smaller than years past. Other things had occupied his mind.

He needed to put his feelings aside long enough to ask Faith why Jean and Tom Rudolph didn't exist on the internet. They may have lived off the grid, but his resources almost always sniffed people out.

SLOANE TROTTED down the front steps with her coat open and flapping behind her. "Aren't you done decorating yet? We can barely walk around the yard." The smile on her face masked the sarcasm she tried to inflict on her tone.

"I don't know if I need something else to beat Davis with." He had checked the status of the best house contest too. Davis was ahead of him by several votes.

"Well, you'd better get it up and fast. That storm is coming. I'm glad Cleo will be off that bus before it hits." She looked up the street at the empty road.

"I've asked Faith to decorate the tree with us." He kept his focus on the oversized ornament.

"Is that some kind of warning that I'd better like her or else?"

"I hope you will like her." He hadn't brought a woman home in ages. There never seemed to be a point. After his divorce, he hadn't looked for anything serious. Something changed this Christmas.

"Why couldn't you fall for someone who didn't come with a luggage rack full of baggage? She might not be capable of anything more than a few nights with you. Are you ready to handle that?" She checked over her shoulder again.

The bus lumbered around the corner. Its engine echoed off the wind. If he stood mute long enough, Cleo would bounce off the bus and Sloane's pointed question would be washed away in stories of kindergarten antics.

"You can avoid my question all you want. But I know you really like this woman. I only hope she's right for you."

The bus slowed but didn't put its lights on.

"What's up with the bus?" he said.

At a complete stop, the doors opened. Mr. Shears with his black-and-red baseball hat smiled a wide tooth-filled grill. "Afternoon, Miss Sloane. I thought

145

you picked little Cleo up at school. She's not on the bus."

The color drained from Sloane's face. "She never got on the bus?"

"No, ma'am. Do you want me to radio the school and see if she missed it?" Mr. Shears already had the radio in his hand before he finished the sentence.

"Thank you. Zane?" She turned to him. "What do I do? Should I call the police? Can Hank help?"

"Don't panic. She probably missed the bus." But the ice water in his blood said something else.

"Ms. Sloane, she isn't there. Someone picked her up this afternoon claiming to be her aunt. Had a note and everything." Mr. Shears pressed his full lips into a thin line.

Sloane howled. He gripped his sister by the arms to keep her from toppling over.

"Sloane, look at me. Call the police. I'll call Hank and go to the school. You stay here in case she hopped in the car with one of her friends." His heart made a mad dash into the panic lane, but he couldn't allow fear to paralyze him.

"But she knows not to get in the car with anyone unless it's me or you." Her voice trembled.

"It's going to be okay." It had to be.

"Find her, Zane."

He would find his niece or die trying.

⁓

DAYLIGHT ENDED, turning the Montana sky a flat black ink absent of stars and the moon. The storm clouds that hung like pregnant cotton sprinkled flakes in angry bursts. The trees swayed to a strong wind. Zane still couldn't find Cleo. The clock ticked away precious minutes.

He pounded on Faith's front door until his knuckles ached. "Open the door."

She was inside. He couldn't understand what was taking so long. He tried the knob, but it was locked.

The door swung inward. "Is everything okay? Did you get another card?" Faith's hair hung loose around her shoulders. She pulled closed the flannel shirt she had swiped from his closet last night.

Last night he loved the idea of her dressed in his clothes, but now the sight of her confused him. He needed answers. "Cleo has been kidnapped. I have to know everything about your parents. Now."

She flinched from the tone in his voice, but he was past caring. It had been hours since anyone had seen Cleo, and every second she was gone only put them closer to the worst possible thing happening. He wouldn't allow that little girl to be hurt. He'd find her, and he needed Faith's help.

"Kidnapped? Oh no. That can't be. What can I do to help?" She reached for her coat.

"Tell me the rest of the story about your parents." He tugged the red envelope out of his pocket and held it up.

He'd found it taped to the fake red-and-green mailbox on his lawn. It was the same card Faith had been getting. This time the note was for him.

"It says 'little girls can get hurt too.' Now you'd better start from the beginning and tell me every detail because my niece is missing, and it's my fucking fault." He had allowed his feelings for Faith to distract him from his job, and now Cleo was in trouble.

She wrung her hands. "I'm so sorry. How is Sloane doing?"

"Hurry up, Faith. I don't have time for your apologies." The terror and anger in his voice startled him as much as it must've Faith.

She stared at him with wide eyes. "Wouldn't it be better if I helped search?"

He slammed his fist on the table by the door. "No. I need details."

Tears filled her eyes. He was being a bastard, but he couldn't stop himself.

"Okay. Um. My parents stole jewelry. I don't know about all the ins and outs. I do know they used the jewelry store as a front. I told you that. They tried to keep it from me, but I figured it out. I was young. A teenager. And angry all the time. The grown-ups weren't honest in my house, but they expected me to follow their rules, tell the truth, all the stupid stuff parents preach. At my age, I didn't want to hear it from them. So, at night after they went to sleep, I would disarm the alarm and sneak out. I did it almost every night of the week. They never suspected. My mother took sleeping pills. My father slept like the dead. I thought I was showing them that they couldn't stop me from living the life I wanted."

"I don't understand what this has to do with anything."

"I'm getting to it."

"Well, hurry up."

"Sure. The night they died, Christmas Day night, I snuck out like usual. I might've been gone a couple of hours. When I came back in, they were dead. I never told anyone about my sneaking out that night. I told the police I was home and slept through the whole thing. Because it was a holiday, no one questioned me." Tears spilled down her cheeks.

"That's the whole story?"

"Someone knew what I was doing. I bragged to too many people. We had a housekeeper and a landscaper who were at the house all the time. My friends all knew. They could've told their parents. Some were friends with mine. I was arrogant and thought my parents were stupid. Whoever killed them knew us. There wasn't forced entry. The police assumed the alarm was never operative. The killer unscrewed all the wiring. Made it look like the alarm had never been used."

"What about records with the alarm company? They can keep track of when the alarm is turned on and off."

"There were no records. It looked like they'd never paid for the service. As far as the alarm company was concerned, my parents installed their equipment, but never activated anything. The killer was someone on the inside. I just don't know who. I'm so sorry."

"Why aren't there any books on the internet by Faith Rudolph? And no jewelry store owners who were murdered by the last name Rudolph? Why is it the best-selling author, Mac Addison, has never been seen?"

Hank ran a check on Faith and found Mac Addison. Addison lead to Faith Rudolph and that lead to Faith Rosalind Karla. The only survivor of Jean and Tom Karla. Jewelry store owners. Suspected crime family dealing in jewelry.

"I've been hiding all these years. Whoever has been sending the cards has come after me before. You must understand that?"

"Why didn't you tell me about your aliases?"

"I didn't think it was important. I'm still the same person."

"You lied to me. You kept important information from me. If I'd known you were dealing with an inside connection, our search would've gone in a different direction. If you had told me your real name, I might've been able to locate your stalker. If I hadn't been sleeping with you, Cleo wouldn't have been taken." His insides shook as the clock continued to tick down the time left to find Cleo.

"I'm so sorry. I never meant for harm to come to you or your family. Please, let me help in some way. I have some money. I could help search. I'll try and make a list of everyone my parents knew socially. It was long ago, but I could try." Tears flowed freely down her face. She didn't even stop to wipe them.

A piece of him wanted to hold her. She had been through too much in her life. No one should find their parents murdered in their home. And she had spent her adult life running from an invisible stalker who could strike at any time. But Cleo was a baby, and she relied on him to keep her safe. His feelings for Faith would have to wither up until he found Cleo or more likely—forever.

"You've done enough. Stay here. Don't get involved. But you might want to pray, because if anything happens to Cleo, so help me God, I'll be back here for you."

## CHAPTER 19

FAITH CLUTCHED HER STOMACH. She should have come completely clean with Zane from the start, but she really believed her name didn't matter much. She secretly hoped whoever was sending the cards would tire of this game.

"I don't have what you want." She shouted inside the empty house.

The wind howled in response shaking the glass in the window panes. Snow dropped from the sky. They had to find Cleo. It was dark and cold. She must be frightened to death and it was all Faith's fault.

She didn't blame Zane for hating her. She wasn't too pleased with herself. There must be something she could do to help, but Zane made it clear she wouldn't be welcomed. It might be better to wait out the storm and pray, like he said. Only she was the reason Cleo was in trouble. She couldn't sit by and do nothing.

She reached for her coat and tugged at the front door. She would join the search. Another set of eyes would be helpful. Or she could pour coffee for the searches. Whatever they needed.

The snow fell in large white clumps, making everything it coated slippery and untouchable. The wind whipped right through her clothes. She stopped mid-step. A red envelope was taped to the railing on the porch. It fought against the wind to keep its place on the pole. The snow wet its edges.

Her breath froze in her lungs. With shaking hands, she pulled the envelope free and tore open the flap secured with tape. Still no DNA. Smart bastards. The same stupid card mocked her as she flipped it open.

*What we want in exchange for the girl. Come alone.* The stalkers included an address and time.

She ran to Zane's and pounded on the front door. The lights were on inside, but no one answered. "Zane. Sloane. Please open up."

They must've left someone behind in case Cleo came back. She tried the knob. It turned under her touch. She hurried inside, not caring if her presence was unwelcomed. She needed Zane's help. Only a stupid person would go alone to meet the kidnappers.

"Zane?" The house was empty. The ticking of the

clock above the kitchen sink cut into the heavy silence.

The kitchen counters were covered in baking supplies. Trays of dough cut in candy cane shapes littered the table. Flour dusted the floor. Fingerprints clouded the stainless-steel oven. Sloane was in the middle of a normal holiday season day when her world blew up.

Faith fought for a controlling breath. She had to make this right and pulled out her phone. The call to Zane rang in her ears unanswered. Of course, he wouldn't pick up her call. "Zane, it's me. I know where Cleo is. Call me."

What she didn't know was what the kidnappers wanted. She jotted a note on a napkin and shoved it under a magnet on the fridge. There was one thing she did have, and she would bring it with her when she went to meet the bastards that had Cleo.

FAITH DRAGGED the two boxes that were the remainder of her past out of the basement corner. She hadn't been down here since the day she moved in. The cold basement matched the ice around her heart. Even her parka couldn't warm her up. The one lightbulb hung naked and alone from the center of the ceiling. Its glow did little to shove away the darkness around the edges of the room.

The night she left her parents' house for good, she stole a gun. Her father had kept a handgun tucked away at the top of a bookshelf only inches from the ceiling. She had never told them she found it. The killers didn't bother with it. Now she had it, and she would bring it with her.

She rummaged past the old Christmas decorations that smelled like must and mold. The gun was at the bottom of the box in a metal case. Her hand slipped around a familiar object, and she pulled it out.

The gold Santa she had loved when she was little smiled up at her. She was never allowed to touch it because it would break. Her mother insisted it was irreplaceable. All she had wanted as a little girl was to hold it and watch it sparkle in the Christmas lights on the tree. She had grabbed the statue at the last minute when she fled her childhood home and threw it in the box with the other stuff.

Now the idea of even keeping any of this junk turned her blood to black frost. Her parents' touch poisoned everything. They had managed to reach from the grave and hurt an innocent little girl too.

She hurled the Santa against the wall. It shattered. Gold pieces rained onto the floor. One glistening piece caught the light and winked. Scrambling over to see, her breath stuck fast to her throat. The sparkle wasn't from the broken gold pieces. A single large, round diamond teetered on the floor and reflected the light in its many facets.

A piece of white paper also lay in the midst of the mess. She reached for the paper with trembling fingers. The corner of the paper stuck to her finger and ripped as she unfolded it.

*Dear Faith,*

*If you're holding this, Dad and I have left the world. I hope we lived long lives. This diamond is for you. It's your nest egg, retirement, or possibly your college fund. We weren't perfect, but we tried. You're holding a twenty carat, GIA certified G/Si. It's worth close to two million at the time I wrote this. Sell it to James Marrs. Or his daughter. They'll know what to do. We always loved you. Forgive us for our mistakes. Mom.*

All this time she'd had what the killers wanted. Her parents must've stolen it. She would make the swap for Cleo. They could take the diamond.

She didn't want it.

# CHAPTER 20

"MOLLY, I've decided what to do about Mac Addison." Faith navigated the snow-covered streets in her little car while she tried to focus on the voicemail message she left. Her wipers worked overtime to keep the windshield clean.

The wheels spun and slipped on the wet ground, but she had to get to the park on the other side of town. She had ten minutes. The gun was in her lap. The diamond was in the glove compartment.

"I'm not telling the publisher the truth. As soon as the book goes to galley, tell them he died. Lie. I don't care. I'm not revealing myself as him. The finished book is in your inbox." She had thrown together the last of the book before Zane had arrived with the bad news and sent it off, ready to be done with it.

She faced the reality she might not make it through the night. Mac Addison would indeed be dead, and it wouldn't matter how bad her book was. And if she survived, she would start over as someone new. Faith Rudolph. Whoever the hell she actually was.

Zane still hadn't called her back. She'd tried him two more times, each time leaving her plan on his voicemail. If he heard her in time, he could bring the cavalry. She had no idea what she was doing in a situation like this one.

She was all Cleo had at the moment. Faith would have to figure out how to get her and save the day. The park came into view. It was just a small thing with a climbing area in the middle and three-person swing set to the side. Two street lights at the entrance of the park offered nothing in the way of light except a small funnel of glow to prove it was snowing. Hers was the only car in the lot. Did that mean they weren't there, or did the park have another entrance? Where was Zane?

She tried him a final time. "Zane, I'm about to go into the park. I hope you get here soon."

The wind tried to shove her back in the car as she fought to get out. The gun sat in her coat pocket and weighed her down, but it also offered the smallest bit of comfort. Though her heart continued to slam into her ribs no matter what kind of protection the gun might give her.

With her hand in her pocket, she followed the path to the center of the park. "Hello?"

Only the call of the wind responded.

They weren't coming. This was a ruse to drag her away from the safety of her house. For some reason, they didn't want to ambush her indoors like her parents but take her out like an animal in the storm. She turned for the car.

"Faith?" A small voice drifted toward her on the wind.

She stopped and strained to hear. "Who's there?"

"Cleo. I'm here." The voice grew louder and with it a small beam of light bounced through the snowflakes.

She let out a long breath but kept her hand on the gun. Cleo and a tall man with a gun pointing at Cleo's head closed the distance between them. Cleo's hood on her purple jacket was up, but snow had coated the fur lining. Faith almost burst with relief when Cleo smiled.

"Are you cold, sweetie?" She kept her gaze locked on Cleo.

"A little. Can we go home now? I miss my mom. And Uncle Zane promised we would decorate the tree." Her tiny voice trembled.

"Do you have what I want?" The man's voice held a familiar tone. She had heard it before. A thousand times in fact. Right in the kitchen of her parents' house.

Her stomach soured. Her parents' best friend had

killed them for that diamond. He had been the closest thing she would ever have to an uncle.

"Jim. How could you take an innocent girl? If she's hurt, I'll kill you myself." James Marrs stood before her. He was the man her mother told her to trust.

"She's fine. I just want the diamond. It belongs to me."

"I don't know what you're talking about." She had planned on handing it over until she saw Jim. He had betrayed them. She would not allow their deaths to be in vain no matter what crimes they had committed. She still loved them.

"Your parents took a twenty carat from a drop we did together. They thought I didn't notice. Your father always thought I was too stupid to pay attention. But he didn't think that when I sat him on his couch and held a gun to his head."

"How could you hurt your best friends? I thought we were your family." The gun grew cold under her hand in her pocket.

"They weren't my friends. We did work together. No one in our business could be friends. You can't trust anyone. That's why I took Cleo. I needed some insurance you'd come with the diamond. Now, where is my diamond?"

"I don't have it. I have nothing of my parents. After they died, I left the house and all the belongings." The snow landed on her eyelashes. She had to blink to be able to see.

"I noticed that. I ransacked the place after you left. But you must have it. You took something. A suitcase. A vase. Anything. It's in there. Your father stole it from me. I know it." His voice shook the highest branches of the trees.

Cleo began to cry.

"Jim, you're scaring her. None of this is necessary. Just let her come to me and we'll go. No one has to be the wiser. I'm the only one who knows about this." The storm continued to dump snow on them. She lost the feeling in her toes.

"That's where you're wrong. Our little lady here knows who I am and can identify me. Unless I get that diamond so I can get a new face and a new life, no one leaves here except me."

"Please be reasonable. Cleo is freezing. At least let me put her in the car with the heat on."

"I'm long past reasonable. I've spent many years suffering for what your parents did. I've been in hiding. I couldn't continue to work in the jewelry business. Someone has to pay for that. Either give me the diamond or it's going to be you and the girl I kill next."

"Killing us isn't the answer. You still won't have the diamond, and now two more people will be dead. The police will never stop looking for a murderer of a child. Her uncle is a very important person. He has connections. Just let us go and this can all end now."

He turned the gun on her. "Shut up. I want what's

rightfully mine. I've waited and planned. I followed you for years, but you always seemed to slip through my fingers. This time I found you and wasn't going to let you go."

"I'm begging you, Jim. Stop this now." Her hand went numb from the cold even though it had been in her pocket. The metal of the gun managed to make her fingers frozen and stiff.

She would only have a second to react, and she wasn't sure she would be able to pull the trigger, but she had to. She and Cleo were on their own. Zane wasn't coming. If they were going to get out of this alive, she would have to act.

With a final deep breath, she yelled, "Cleo, duck."

The kickback from her pistol threw her off balance. A flash of light blinded her. A pain shot through her shoulder and the power of a locomotive knocked her on her back. Screams filled the sulfur-smelling air.

She fought to get up and get to Cleo, but the pain made her stomach roll. She tried to get to her side to vomit but wasn't sure if she made it. If this were a book she wrote, the hero would arrive right around now and she would help him save the day.

But this was real life.

And she was about to black out.

# CHAPTER 21

ZANE SLAMMED on the brakes in his driveway. He needed to get back to the search for Cleo. With all the teams of volunteers, and Hank's power, she still wasn't found. What kind of criminals were these people?

He had fallen down the embankment near the lake when someone shouted that they thought they saw a body. It was a false alarm. Both a good thing and a bad.

His legs were soaked. He had wanted to keep looking, but Linc ordered him to go home and change before he ended up with hypothermia. The storm had made it almost impossible to drive in. He should've stayed and let the frost bite be damned. He wanted his niece back.

But he wouldn't do anyone any good if he got hurt. He had learned that lesson the hard way in the past. He pushed out of the truck and wanted to tear down all the decorations. How stupid could he have been to think a contest about lights was important?

The only thing that was important was family. Faith had been right to dislike Christmas. He would never celebrate Christmas again if anything happened to Cleo. On a long breath, he unlocked the front door.

"Cheyenne, are you here?" He called into the vast house.

Dr. Cheyenne Locklear, his partner Quint's wife, stuck her head out of the first-floor office. "Hey, what are you doing back?"

Quint had asked Cheyenne to come over and wait in case Cleo showed up.

"What time did you get here?" he said.

"About thirty minutes ago. Not long after you all left. I came as fast as I could, but the snow made it tough, and I was in the middle of a cow giving birth. I'm so sorry about all of this."

"Thanks. I need to change and get back out there."

"I'll make you some coffee to go." She pressed her lips together in a half-smile and headed for the kitchen.

He took the steps two at a time. He shouldn't have yelled at Faith earlier. It wasn't her fault that these people were after her. He'd seen enough to know criminals would do anything to get what they wanted. Cleo was collateral damage to these monsters. If he got the chance, he'd apologize. She might not want to hear it, and he wouldn't blame her. They had a good thing for about a minute. It was too bad it wouldn't last. No other woman had ever grabbed his attention like she did.

In dry clothes, he ran into the kitchen. Cheyenne held a piece of paper. She raised her gaze to meet his. Her mouth fell open. "You'd better read this."

The room spun as he read Faith's note. The paper fell to the floor. "Call Quint. Tell him where I went."

He ran before she could say anything. He didn't know how long ago Faith left that letter. He'd been ignoring all her calls and wanted to kick his ego for its willful pride.

Now he might be too late.

## CHAPTER 22

Zane threw the truck in park and leapt from the seat hoping his arrival would interrupt whatever might be happening. The snow came down in sheets blocking his view into the park. The cold wind froze the inside of his nose before he could take a step and buffered any sounds with its wailing force.

He didn't know what he was running into and didn't care all that much. He pulled his gun from the holster and the small flashlight from his belt to help him see.

His heart pounded in his ears as he went deeper into the park. What if he was too late? He would never be able to explain to Sloane that he had allowed his emotions to interfere.

The flashlight beam swept the area in front of him. A small body in a purple coat lay slumped over another. A female on her back. Her brown hair fanned out as if she might be asleep. The small body didn't move. His heart lodged in his throat, but he forced his legs forward. The snow crunched under his boots. He had to see with his own eyes.

If something had happened to Cleo, he would be the one to tell Sloane. He wouldn't allow anyone else to deliver the news. A third body, male, lay prone on the ground ten yards away. Snow left a thin layer of dust on the man's chest.

He inched forward. "Cleo?" His word was a whisper.

She raised her little head and stared at him. "Uncle Zane?" She blinked against the glare from the flashlight.

He tossed it aside and scooped her up with one arm. The breath left his lungs in a whoosh. "Are you hurt?"

"No. Faith has a big boo-boo. She won't wake up." Tears made streaks in her dirty face. She wrapped her arms around his neck in a death grip.

His heart swelled further and stuck in his throat worse. "I'm going to put you down so I can take a look at Faith and the other man."

She clung harder.

"It's okay." He hoped it would be okay, but Cleo would be affected by this forever.

He kept one eye on the man and lowered Cleo to the ground. The guy didn't budge. With Cleo behind him and clinging to his leg, he approached with his gun drawn. He kicked the man's leg. No response. He felt for a pulse. Nothing.

He grabbed Cleo in his arms to get her away from the dead man. Cars, trucks, and sirens screeched into the parking lot, lighting up the small park like New York City's Times Square. Bud Lewis barreled forward.

"Give her to me. Hey, pretty girl. It's your mommy's friend Bud. You remember me?" Bud pulled Cleo from his arms and met Sloane running toward them. Bud held both ladies while Sloane cried.

Lincoln, Jax, and Quint ran into the park, guns drawn, with Hank, many of the Brotherhood Protectors, and the rest of Winter's police force.

He needed to get back to Faith.

"Dead," Jax said, squatting over the guy on the ground.

"Faith?" He dropped down beside her. Blood covered most of her coat. The snow gathered in her hair. He brushed some away from her face.

"She's got a pulse. Weak, but existent. Let's get her out of here." Linc ordered people around and helped get Faith onto the gurney. "Are you going to ride with her?" Linc said.

"Zane?" Faith's hoarse voice was swallowed up by the wind.

"I'm right here." He grabbed her cold hand and laced his fingers through hers, willing her to know how much she meant to him. He blinked away tears trying to form.

"I didn't think you'd come. Cleo?" She coughed out each word. The dark circle on her coat spread wider.

"She's fine. Don't talk right now. We're going to take you to the hospital. Mind if I come along?"

She closed her eyes but didn't answer.

He climbed into the ambulance.

THE SUN nudged Zane from his sleep. He turned away from the window and reached for Faith. The bed was empty. He sat up.

He had gone with her to the hospital. She had been nicked by the bullet from James Marrs. The docs had stitched her up and sent her home the next morning. He had stayed by her side the entire time.

When she was released, he insisted she stay with him. She hadn't argued. He took that as a sign they might have a chance. Last night, he climbed into bed with her and held her all night. In the early hours of the morning, she accepted his apology, and they made love. He slept without a nightmare for the first time in years.

"Faith?" He threw his legs over the bed and pulled on a pair of sweatpants.

The house was quiet. Sloane and Cleo were out

taking advantage of the early Christmas shopping hours. Cleo had told Hank and the police everything that had happened. Marrs had an old girlfriend pick Cleo up from school. They took her for hot chocolate and went ice skating. He never really wanted to hurt Cleo. He wanted that damn diamond. He got more than he bargained for. He got a coffin and six feet below the earth's surface.

The coffee pot was warm, and a used pod was still in the holder. She couldn't be far. He wished she had woken him. The mystery might be over, but he wasn't ready to leave her alone just yet. She was capable of taking care of herself, but he was a Protector. It was his job, and he wanted to take care of her for a long time.

He grabbed his parka and went outside. The cold morning hit him in the face. "Faith?"

"Over here."

He rounded the front of the house and stopped. "What are you doing?"

She stood on a ladder, decorating a Christmas tree that hadn't been in the yard before. "I'm finishing your decorations. The contest closes tonight. You might still have a chance." She raised her arm over her head and winced.

"Come here." He helped her down the ladder. "You might open up that wound."

"I'm fine. I don't know if what I'm doing will help you win, but I had to try. Lincoln brought the tree over for me this morning, and I had the decorations."

He took a closer look at the tree. The decorations were from another era. They were worn in places from years of use. "Are these your old ornaments?"

"I hung them for you. These last days have been the best days I've had at Christmastime. Minus the kidnapping, of course."

"And being shot." He pulled her close.

"That wasn't fun, but it pales in comparison to what could've happened to Cleo. I wanted you to know how much you mean to me. You make me want to celebrate Christmas again." She looked up at him with warmth in her eyes.

"I can't imagine spending Christmas with anyone else. Thank you for sharing your decorations. I know that was hard for you, but I don't care if I win anymore. I realized the only thing that matters to me is having my family around. I want that to include you too. If you'll have me." He ran his thumb over her jaw and savored the ease of being with her.

"I like the sound of that."

"I have to ask you something," he said.

"Anything."

"What are you going to do with that diamond?" The statute of limitations on grand larceny had passed. In the eyes of the law, she was innocent, and so were her parents.

"Would you be against the idea of a foundation

for victims of violent crimes and their families? And maybe a college fund for Cleo?"

"Those sound like great ideas. And what about your book? Did you ever get through to your agent?" The snow began to fall again and dusted their shoulders, but he didn't move. As long as he had Faith in his arms, he'd be warm.

"No more hiding. I'm doing the book tour, but not till after the new year. I want to spend these next weeks with you by the Christmas tree."

"I like the sound of that." He echoed her words.

She wrapped her arms around his neck and kissed him. He cupped the back of her head to take the kiss deeper, and she rewarded him with a soft moan. They were at the start of what could be a wonderful journey. He couldn't wait for their adventures to begin.

"We'll take that competition hands down next year." She eased back and met his gaze.

"Davis won't know what hit him."

"We can use both yards." Her eyes sparkled like a star on the top of the tree.

"Merry Christmas, Faith."

"Merry Christmas, Zane."

# ABOUT STACEY WILK

Stacey Wilk wrote her first novel in middle school to quiet the characters in her head. It was that or let them out to eat the cannolis, and she wasn't sharing her grandfather's Italian pastries.

Many years later her life took an adventurous turn when she gave birth to two different kinds of characters. She often sits in awe of their abilities to roll their eyes, stay-up all hours of the night, and misplace everything. She does share the cannolis with them for fear of having her fingers bitten off.

Because of the extraordinary characters in her home, including a king who surfaces after dark and for coffee, she writes novels in multiple genres about family, home, and second chances.

When she's not creating stories in make-believe places, she can be found hanging with the cast members of her house or teaching others how to make make-believe worlds of their own.

Stop by for a visit and make sure to bring some cannolis.
www.staceywilk.com

Or her private Facebook group for her amazing readers – Stacey's Novel Family
http://bit.ly/NovelFamily

Or her newsletter - http://bit.ly/FamilyUChoose

BROTHERHOOD PROTECTORS

ORIGINAL SERIES BY ELLE JAMES

*Brotherhood Protectors Series*

Montana SEAL (#1)

Bride Protector SEAL (#2)

Montana D-Force (#3)

Cowboy D-Force (#4)

Montana Ranger (#5)

Montana Dog Soldier (#6)

Montana SEAL Daddy (#7)

Montana Ranger's Wedding Vow (#8)

Montana SEAL Undercover Daddy (#9)

Cape Cod SEAL Rescue (#10)

Montana SEAL Friendly Fire (#11)

Montana SEAL's Mail-Order Bride (#12)

SEAL Justice (#13)

Ranger Creed (#14)

Delta Force Strong (#15)

Montana Rescue (Sleeper SEAL)

Hot SEAL Salty Dog (SEALs in Paradise)

Hot SEAL Hawaiian Nights (SEALs in Paradise)

## ABOUT ELLE JAMES

ELLE JAMES also writing as MYLA JACKSON is a *New York Times* and *USA Today* Bestselling author of books including cowboys, intrigues and paranormal adventures that keep her readers on the edges of their seats. With over eighty works in a variety of sub-genres and lengths she has published with Harlequin, Samhain, Ellora's Cave, Kensington, Cleis Press, and Avon. When she's not at her computer, she's traveling, snow skiing, boating, or riding her ATV, dreaming up new stories. Learn more about Elle James at www.ellejames.com

Website | Facebook | Twitter | GoodReads | Newsletter | BookBub | Amazon

*Follow Elle!*
www.ellejames.com
ellejames@ellejames.com

facebook.com/ellejamesauthor
twitter.com/ElleJamesAuthor